ROSE M. COOPER

Published by Oshun Publications
9 Old Kings Road STE. 123-1038
Palm Coast, FL 32137
www.oshunpublications.com

Book Design by oliviaprodesign
www.fiverr.com/oliviaprodesign

ISBN 978-1-950378-61-6 (Paperback)
ISBN 978-1-956319-37-8 (Hardback)
ISBN 978-1-950378-60-9 (eBook)

Also by Rose M. Cooper

Can't Buy a Billionaire Series

A Virgin for the Bachelor Billionaire

Training the Billionaire

One Night with the Billionaire

The Billionaire's Bet

The Billionaire and the Biker Chick

The Billionaire's Billboard Proposal

Bobsledding with the Billionaire

Snowed In With the Billionaire

Accidentally Married to Her Billionaire Boss

Bought by the Billionaire

Bargaining with the Billionaire

Persuaded by the Billionaire

Unmasking the Billionaire

Romancing the Billionaire

ROSEMAECOOPER.COM

THERE ARE ALSO AUDIOBOOKS!

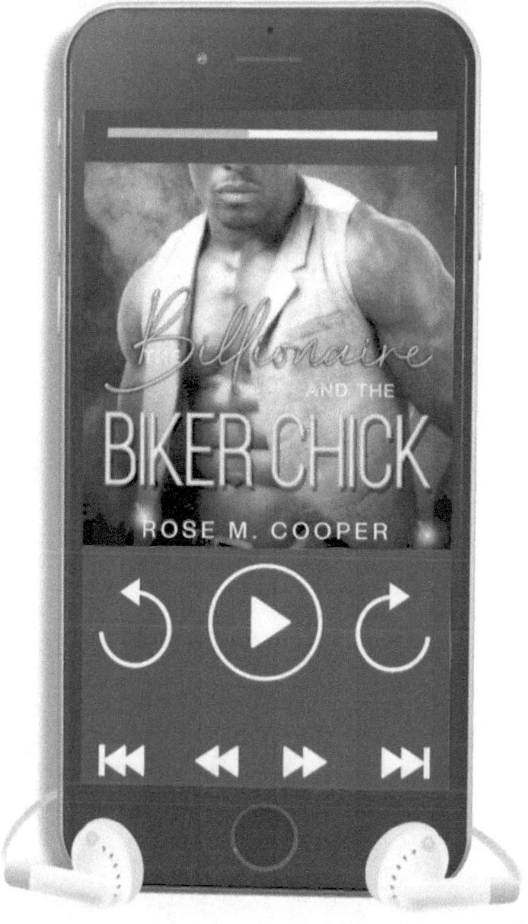

rosemaecooper.com/audiobooks

CHAPTER 1

To Relive a Dream

Little beads of perspiration gleamed off Jordan Turner's well-defined arms. He threw a few jab-right crosses and then jab-cross-left uppercut-cross shadow boxing combinations. His upper body was relaxed, his spine straight but well-controlled as he moved his feet nimbly across the mat. His six-foot-three frame moved effortlessly while he made sure the filming cameras got in the shots of the gear and championship fight he was promoting.

"That's a wrap," the young video producer told his small team that had joined him at Jordan's home training gym.

"Thank you once again, Mr. Turner, for allowing us to film this in your gym." The young producer smiled, a little star-struck. Jordan Turner was a legend in the boxing world. "My younger brother is a boxer and has always been inspired by your career."

"It is always nice to hear that I can still inspire the youth of today." Jordan laughed, taking a sip of water.

"May I ask why you quit, especially when you were at the top of your game, unbeaten?" the young man asked Jordan.

A shadow came across his eyes. "I was at the age where I felt it was time for a change," Jordan said, wiping his damp body and arms with a fluffy blue towel. "To be honest, I have had the itch to return to competing for the past couple of months."

"Oh, wow," the young man said, beaming with delight, "that would be awesome; your fans would go nuts."

"Or they would think I was having an early mid-life crisis!" Jordan laughed, running the towel through his damp hair again.

"I know you probably get this all the time," the young man said sheepishly, "but it would mean the world to my brother if he could meet you."

"Sure." Jordan smiled. "No problem. On your way out, ask Quinton, my agent, for my card."

"That is so great," his young face glowed with excitement, "I can't wait to tell my brother." He walked off to go gather up the camera crew and check the equipment.

"They will check the footage and come back to you for the final review," Quinton informed Jordan after letting the camera crew out. "I had an interesting conversation with the young editor," he continued, raising an eyebrow at his client, who also happened to be one of his oldest friends. "He tells me you are thinking about getting back into boxing."

"He told you that?" Jordan walked through the gym into the shower room. "Or did you overhear that while skulking around in the shadows?" He laughed and threw his dirty towel at Quinton.

"Fine." Quinton fought off the disgusting towel. "I overheard the two of you talking, and the young man was eager to know if it were true. Well?"

"To be honest," Jordan began, as he sat down on the bench to untie the laces of his boxing boots, "I have been thinking about it more and more."

"Come on, Jordan," Quinton leaned back against a locker, "we have been over this. You left the boxing world at the top of your game. Why risk your reputation now?"

"That's the thing, Quint," Jordan pulled off his boots, tossing them into the shoe basket, "I think I got out too early. I feel like I never really got to prove myself or go as far as I wanted to go."

"But look at all you have accomplished since you retired from boxing," Quinton told him. "You are still one of the top male sports models, and let's face it, at thirty, that is a huge compliment."

"Gosh, thanks," Jordan replied, his brow furrowed, "but I think most of the sports companies come to me to ensure I don't start producing my own line of their specialized goods."

"Maybe," Quinton laughed, and then he nimbly dodged a friendly punch thrown at him. "You are still boxing's darling pretty boy." He patted Jordan on the back, instantly regretting it when his hand came into contact with Jordan's sweat-soaked shirt.

"You know I have one more belt to add to my wall," said Jordan, as he pictured his trophy room.

"Why?" Quinton shook his head, "You already hold three of the four major championship belts, which is an incredible achievement."

"I feel there is still a lot more for me to accomplish." Jordan sighed and continued, "I thought the boxing light burned out for me the night Wayne died. But I think I was fooling myself as the light only dulled." His voice dropped to almost a whisper.

"You have to stop beating yourself up about your brother's death," Quinton told Jordan. "Getting over a loved one's death never leaves us; it is always there, but then so are they. We carry them with us in our memories."

"Wow. That's rather deep. Even for you!" Jordan laughed as a telltale red stained Quinton's cheeks.

"Yeah, I lost someone recently, so I know." Quinton gave Jordan a tight smile. "I may not have been that close to my father as I would have liked, but the fact remains, he was still my father."

"I know, buddy," said Jordan, giving Quinton's arm a pat. "It's hard not to think of being able to pick up the phone to call them or not find a message from them."

"Although I never got those from my dad." Quinton smiled; sadly, ", there was always the possibility of getting one while he was still alive. Now, well, I never will, and if I did, well, I would be the first one looking for a priest."

The two men looked at each other and burst into laughter.

"Well, I am going to leave you to clean up because you stink, man," Quinton said, wrinkling his nose. "And I tell you this as your best friend." He ducked as a dirty sock was hurtled at his head as he left the locker room.

"Okay," Quinton said as he leaned back into the comfortable sofa, a slice of pizza in his hand. "So tell me again, why are you hell-bent on this stupid idea of getting back in the ring?"

"I told you," Jordan shrugged, ignoring the tantalizing smell of the pizza sitting on his glass coffee table. "I feel like I have more to accomplish."

"You know I think you are completely crazy, right?" Quinton said, biting into his pizza slice. "But I get it. Although I must say, you are rather out of shape for a boxer," he added, glancing at Jordan's midsection. Quinton grinned as he munched on his food, nearly choking when the thrown sofa pillow met his face.

"I realize that." Jordan gave in to the pizza temptation. "The last woman I was with told me the same thing."

"What, that you were losing your mind?" Quinton laughed, getting another whack with a pillow.

"Out of shape." Jordan eyed the gooey mess he was about to take a bite of. "Something about me being in the beginning of a dad's bod." He thought about not eating the slice in his hand, shrugged, and took a bite anyway.

"If this is what you're set on, you know you're going to need a trainer," Quinton told him.

"I want the best. I *need* the best, and old Vic passed away a few years ago," Jordan replied.

"I heard." Quinton watched him. "So unless you have an Ouija board, he's no longer available."

"I know. It was a shock," said Jordan as he took another bite of his pizza. "He was a good man."

"That he was," Quinton replied, agreeing with Jordan. "He certainly boosted your career in a major way," Quinton felt no guilt in taking another slice of pizza.

"I know of a few trainers out there who may be interested in helping you revive your boxing career," Quinton told Jordan. "Having you as a client would be a feather in their hat. I can give them a call in the morning while I work on some tournaments for you."

"Thanks, but keep working on the tournaments," Jordan wiped his hands on a napkin. "I already have a trainer in mind."

"Oh?" Quinton stopped mid-pizza bite, his eyebrows raised questioningly.

CHAPTER 2
Holding on to a Legacy

"KEEP YOUR FIST UP; protect your face," Skye yelled over the squeaking vinyl flooring as she watched the young man spar with one of her gym members. "Footwork, Mason; remember the lines. That's good, not too close to your opponent."

"How is he doing?" Mason's father approached her as silently as a cat, making her jump.

"Oh, hi, Carter," Skye said, smiling up at the tall man; he was a retired MMA fighter whom her father had once trained. "Mason is doing well. He needs to keep working on his foot drills, and he drops his left hand a lot."

"I will work on that with him," said Carter, smiling down at her. "I appreciate you doing this for us. He so wants to cage-fight, but his mother would haunt me if I let him."

"I can understand that." Skye turned and smiled at Carter before returning her attention to the ring. "Although my father encouraged me to do what I wanted to do, he had reservations about me boxing." She grimaced as she watched Joey, her gym hand, land a punch, knocking Mason backward. "Excuse me a minute."

Skye hopped into the boxing ring. Telling Joey to take five, she worked on Mason's posture and footwork.

"I think that is enough for today," Skye told the young man. "You have made remarkable progress, Mason. You have to keep working on keeping up your left hand."

"Yeah, about that..." Mason rolled his left shoulder. "I have been feeling pain again in my shoulder from the operation after my skiing accident."

"Didn't the physiotherapist clear you almost seven months ago?" Skye asked the young man, who nodded while she felt his shoulder and tested his range of motion. "When did it start hurting again?"

"A couple of weeks ago." Mason shrugged. "It was during football practice. I went to throw the ball downfield, and it felt like something hot was ripping through my flesh."

"Did you tell your dad?" Skye worked her fingers along Mason's intrinsic muscles and felt him flinch. "You are going to need to go to the doctor, Mason." Skye told him as she put his arm down, "I can't let you train like this, and you need to cool it with football until the doctor clears you."

"Why didn't you tell me?" Carter's voice came to them from the side of the ring, making them both jump.

"You were so excited that I made quarterback this year, Dad," Mason bowed his head. "I didn't want to disappoint you."

"Son," Carter said as he hopped into the ring, "I, more than anyone, know how not treating an injury can impact your sporting career. I've told you that nothing is more important than your health. Everything else comes second."

"Would you like me to get Mason in with Carly?" Skye asked Carter, referring to one of the top sports medicine specialists in the country, who just also happened to be her best friend. “I am sure she would be happy to see Mason again.”

“Please, Skye, we would appreciate it.” Carter sighed.

“No.” Mason jumped in. “Please, dad, I have a big game coming up. It will be okay; I can’t miss the first game of the season. I just can’t.”

“Mason,” Skye said gently. “You tore your rotator cuff in that skiing accident eighteen months ago and had major surgery on it. It is now a weak point that you need to take proper care of.” Skye smiled at him. “Just go have it looked at. In the meantime, ice your shoulder down and don’t do anything that can put stress on it. I do mean anything.”

“I will see to it. Thank you, Skye.” Carter smiled at her. “Come on, son, let’s get you home.”

“I will have Carly call you and set up the appointment,” Skye said as she waved them out of the gym, smiling.

Skye’s heart felt so heavy for them. Mason had lost his mother, and Carter, the love of his life, three years ago. Now, Carter dedicated every spare moment he had to taking care of his son. Sometimes, he may have been overprotective.

“That was a tough break, that accident,” Joey quipped, helping Skye pack away gym equipment that had been left out. “Rotator cuffs are like Achilles’ tendons; once they have been weakened, they tend to always give problems.”

“Speaking of Achilles’ tendons,” Skye said, dragging a giant mat and plunking it into place. “How is the ankle?”

“I am back in the league.” Joey wiggled his foot to show Skye. “Fingers crossed, it has not given any trouble these past weeks.”

Skye eyed the movement. “That’s great news.”

“I have my first MMA fight in two weeks. Please don’t forget. You know you are my lucky charm.”

“You know I would never miss one of your fights,” Skye told the young man, laughing. “How many have I missed?”

"Two." Joey grinned, but a dark shadow flicked across his eye. "And that was only because of Uncle Vic."

Clearing her throat, "Are you ready?" Skye changed the subject; she still could not believe her father had passed away.

Skye's father's death had left such a massive hole in her heart, in her life, and in the business. Over two years later, that hole was still as big as it was the day he passed away. Everyone at the gym missed him.

"Are you kidding me?" Joey laughed. "I have this ferocious trainer who is also my boss. She would literally kick my butt if I lost."

"Very funny." Skye punched him on the arm. "Speaking of which, I have your new gear for the fight. It arrived earlier today."

"Really?" Joey's eyes lit up. "Can I have a look?" He followed Skye into her back office.

"Here you go." Skye picked up a box and handed it to him. "Thank you for still wanting to wear the gym's name and colors."

"Of course." Joey pulled out the gear. "I'm representing not only the gym but you and Uncle Vic." Feeling the short's microfiber fabric, he smiled and said, "I am going to look awesome, Skye. I know you could not afford to do this, so it is very special that you did. No matter what endorsements I get, this gym will always have a place on my fighting gear."

"Yeah." Skye smiled at him. "I will hold you to that when you win the championship this year."

"I just know this year is my year," said Joey as he walked to the door, stopping at the entrance. "Do you think Carter would be willing to give me a few tips?"

"I can ask him for you when I set up an appointment for him with Carly if you like?" Skye offered.

"That would be so awesome." Joey ran back into the office to give her a giant hug, picking her up and spinning her around. "You are the best boss ever," he said in his amateur rapper voice before running off, his new gear stashed beneath his very-toned arms.

Skye shook her head as she watched the young man leave. She sat back in the chair that once belonged to her father. The usual lump swelled in her throat as she thought about him. He was a great man who had left her big shoes to fill. She eyed the pile of bills stacked on her desk that she needed to address and couldn't help but feel she was failing him.

"This a bad time?" Bennie, her only other employee now at the gym, gave a light knock on the door frame.

"No, not at all." Skye swiped at the moisture at the corner of her eyes. Clearing her throat, she announced, "Come on in. I was hoping to catch you before you left. As you may have noticed, Joey left here at the speed of light."

"I saw. He was distracting me from the group class by bragging with his new gear," Bennie said, laughing. He had been with Vic's Gym for forty years. Skye's father had lifted him out of a bad place, given him a home and a purpose when he was eighteen. "I really think that kid should be boxing, not doing all that MMA stuff."

"He is a good fighter," Skye agreed with Bennie, "but the kid loves MMA. His heart is not in full-time boxing."

"Such a shame," replied Bennie, shaking his head. "Such a waste of great talent."

"He is still young. He could still go pro boxing if he wanted to." Skye twirled her pen. "But, as you know, when your heart is set on a path, it is hard to change it. It becomes almost an obsession."

"You should know. Your father taught you well, Skye," Bennie told her.

Bennie's brown eyes shone with pride for the young woman Skye had become. He had watched her grow up, and she was like a daughter to him and the closest thing he had to family. Bennie would do anything for her.

"That is very sweet," Skye said, sighing as she leaned her elbows on the desk and ran her hand through her hair. "I am so scared we may have to close down dad's gym or, at the very least, move it to a cheaper location."

"Hey." Bennie reached over to pat her hand affectionately. "You will make it work. I know you. You are as stubborn as your father was. If not more so."

"I hope so, Bennie." She smiled sadly. "I really hope so."

"I wish you would let me help you," said Bennie, shaking his head as her jaw set stubbornly. "What good is all this money I have saved up over the years if I can't help out my family?"

"Because you are retiring in three years and want to go to Florida." Skye raised her eyebrows at him. "But thank you, Bennie. It was a great comfort having you around when Dad passed away. I know you were planning to take early retirement four years ago."

"No way would I ever leave my girl in the lurch," Bennie said, smiling warmly at her. "Now, let's discuss the afternoon group classes for next week. I also have some ideas on how to bring in more clients."

Skye was distracted as she let herself into her apartment above the gym. Her father had bought the entire building thirty years ago. But rising costs and losing their star boxer five years ago had forced her father to take out a mortgage on the building. Keeping up with those payments proved decidedly tricky, along with staff costs, utility bills, equipment repairs, and modern gym trends and protocols. There were endless equipment, as well as the building to get up to code, and this license, then that license became a never-ending cycle of bills.

Vic's Gym was barely keeping afloat when her father was alive. But he still had a full gym with regular paying clients. Her father's coaching reputation drew in a lot of top boxers and potential new talent. When he died, the gym had lost nearly all its regular paying clients. Other than a few loyal customers whom Skye, Bennie, and Joey had trained while her father was alive, the rest had stopped coming to Vic's Gym. Those departing customers did not feel that a woman had any business in the fighting world. Most of the top trainers who worked for her father felt the same way and left. The other trainers who had stuck by her, she was forced to let go due to lack of funds.

She kicked off her trainers at the door, as she always did. Stopping in the living room, Skye looked around the apartment she had grown up in. There were so many memories. The realtor who had come to see her the other day suggested she rent this apartment out. It was a nice-sized three-bedroom apartment in an up-and-coming area of the city, where the property was currently highly sought-after. She was seriously thinking about that idea. It would mean that Bennie could retire and move to Florida, as he and his late wife Amelia had planned to do. She could move into the bachelor apartment that Bennie now occupied.

When Skye's father passed away, Bennie cleared out the bachelor pad that they used as a storeroom and moved in to keep an eye on Skye. There was another apartment on the ground floor, with two bedrooms and a nice sized garden located at the gym's back. Bennie and his wife Amelia had lived there since before Skye was born, and Bennie started working for her father. She could remember many days spent in that garden with Amelia and Bennie. She loved to help plant herbs and vegetables. All their family holiday barbeques were held there. Then there was the small private pool she spent her summers splashing about in.

It had been awful having to take Bennie up on his offer that they rent out his apartment and fix up the smaller one next door to hers for him. She felt like all those memories the apartment held were being swept away as strangers replaced them with the home they would make there. That apartment and the one she was standing in were her homes. When Amelia passed away ten years ago, Skye lost the only mother she had ever known. But every time she walked into that apartment, it was like walking into Amelia's arms. Just like her and her father's apartment kept her close to him.

The steady income from the rental of Bennie's apartment to a single mother of twin boys was what kept the lights on at the gym. If it wasn't for the diner across the road where she and Bennie ate every night, she would probably have starved by now. She had known the diner owners her entire life. Her new menu suggestions had stopped the diner from having to close, and now Urban City Kitchen had waiting lists for tables. They also expanded their business to make daily meals for top sports stars, celebrities, and business executives. Skye always had a table waiting for her, and her meals were made for her every day at no cost.

Skye sighed; renting out the apartment would be a lot better than having to lose the gym altogether. She padded through to the kitchen to put her premade diner breakfast in the refrigerator. Apart from bottled water, there was nothing else in the appliance. She pulled open the freezer section and pulled out her frozen Tiramisu that Maggie O'Brien, the baker down the road, made for Skye once a week. The O'Brien's bakery had been in the neighborhood for three O'Brien generations. Maggie's daughter, Carly, was also Skye's best friend and one of the top sports injury doctors in the state, if not the country. Maggie and Skye's father had been unofficially together since Skye was about ten. They both had commitment issues; Skye guessed that was why they never married.

Skye pulled the dessert from the freezer; she loved it icy because the fresh cream it was made of stayed fresh. It was ice cream tiramisu; she giggled to herself while grabbing a spoon before padding over to the lounge. She checked the answering machine; there were no messages, so she grabbed her mobile phone before flopping down on the sofa.

She was going to sit on the sofa, watch some mindless show on TV, eat her dessert, and play Candy Crush on her phone. She flicked on the TV, tuning in to her favorite Spanish telenovela. Upon the insistence of her father, Skye had taken Spanish and French at school. She found she had a knack for languages and was pretty fluent in both. Besides, who didn't love the drama of a telenovela?

Skye wiped her eyes; she had showered about ninety minutes ago and changed into her pajamas when the telenovela had finished. Now she watched a Hallmark romance movie with a bowl of microwave popcorn and a bottle of soda she had gotten from Bennie. She did love a light-hearted romance movie, especially when she could not sleep as her mind was too full of worries.

Bennie was always on at her about going out and enjoying herself. He would say that she needed to see the world, spread her wings, and maybe even fall in love. The truth was, Skye was where she needed to be for now—and falling in love, well, that was not on her to-do list for anytime soon, not after the last fiasco. And she was definitely never going to date a sports star again either. Their egos were the only relationships they needed in their lives; everyone else was just food that nourished those egos.

Skye shuddered at the thought of Declan Bell, her ex-fiancé who was a pro football player. He was one guy she hoped not to run into any time soon, especially not while the gym was struggling. Skye could just hear him sneer at her now.

"I told you being a trainer was no job for you. This is for men, like your dad."

Idiot, he had become so swept away with the fame and groupies that he had gone from a reasonably decent guy to one she could not bear to be in the same room with. Well, there was only space for him and his ego in a room anyway.

Skye was so deep in thought that she nearly fell off the sofa when her phone rang. She picked it up, frowning. It was a number she did not recognize. She hesitated for a moment, looking at the clock on the wall. It was after ten. Would a company call about overdue bills so late at night?

"Hello," Skye answered the phone, her heart hammering in her chest as she waited for a customer service representative to reply.

"Is this Skye Larsen?" A deep, familiar voice boomed through the earpiece.

"Yes, this is Skye," she said hesitantly.

"Hi." The deep voice became less formal. "This is Jordan Turner; your father used to be my trainer."

"I know who you are," Skye said flatly, her voice belying the hammering of her heart.

"Sorry for calling you so late," the voice on the other line said. She could all but hear the charming smile he must have on his face emanate from his voice. "I have a business proposition for you. Can we meet tomorrow at my place?"

CHAPTER 3
A Tempting Offer

SKYE LOOKED around Jordan's house. It was what you would expect from one of the most eligible bachelors around. A lot of sparkling clean windows looking out over manicured rolling lawns and a swimming pool surrounded by expensive patio furniture.

Skye bet he had not chosen one item outside or inside his house by himself. She looked around the living room she had been ushered into; there were soft overstuffed leather sofa and chairs with a glass and chrome coffee table. Jordan's decorator obviously loved minimalism, as there was not much in the room.

The fireplace was nice, though. It was one of those modern ones that could be turned on by remote control from anywhere inside the house or away from the home. Skye looked at the control panel on the wall. She could not understand people's attraction to smart houses.

She shuddered; her car with all its electronic gadgets was enough. Skye always felt like it was watching her and judging her. She had that same feeling being in a smart house; it freaked her out. Creepy! She thought absently as she rubbed away the gooseflesh that had popped up on her skin.

There were no photographs in this room, only one picture of some abstract sort of art hanging over the fireplace. Skye stood, looking at the art. It was weird that it looked like a whole breadstick randomly stacked together.

"It's Claire White," Jordan said from the door to the living room, making her jump, as he had snuck up so quietly. "It is her depiction of how one's soul slowly shrinks with every life knock they take."

"Awesome." Skye shook her head in amazement that someone would see that from that mesh of breadsticks.

Skye turned to look at Jordan; her heart fluttered, and her belly knotted. Jordan's six-foot-three frame filled the sparsely furnished room, his t-shirt clinging to his body and outlining his muscled torso. His dark brown hair was expertly cut to accentuate his ruggedly handsome face and brown eyes. She could smell the freshly showered scent of him from four feet away.

"It is so good to see you, Skye," Jordan said as he walked into the room, enveloping her in a hug. "I was so sorry to hear about your father." He stood back, holding her upper arms as he offered his condolences.

"Thank you," Skye said coolly, politely stepping out of his embrace. "May I ask what I am doing here?" She thought she may as well get straight to the point. The quicker she could get out, the better.

"I can see you are a lot like your father, too," Jordan laughed. "Straight down to business, as time spent gabbling is time taken away from training."

"My father did like to use that line a lot." Skye's features softened, relaxing a bit as she thought about her father. "I have had to adopt that attitude these days with a business to run."

"Yes, of course," Jordan said, taking a seat and indicating for her to do the same. "I won't keep you long then."

Skye sat down in a chair across the coffee table from Jordan. His clean male scent was wreaking havoc with her senses; he was still a very sexy man. Skye gave herself a mental shake.

No more dating jocks; remember your pact to never ever date an athlete ever again! Big egos, big heartache! Skye iterated in her mind. They were just too high maintenance, and it was tough being in a relationship where you had to compete with a guy's ego. Or, in Jordan's case, she would not want to be his female companion of the week.

"Can I offer you some refreshments?" Jordan asked her.

"No, thank you," Skye politely declined, sitting back in the chair and hoping the giant cushions wouldn't swallow her tiny frame. She felt like she was sitting in a giant's chair.

"To answer your question as to why I asked you here today," Jordan smiled warmly at her, sitting back comfortably on the sofa, "I am looking for a coach. I only want the best, and I believe that since your father passed, that torch has been passed down to you."

"Uh, thank you?" Skye frowned at him, both a little flattered by his compliment and suspicious of what he was offering. "Are you sponsoring a new boxer?" She asked him curiously.

"No." Jordan smiled at her. "You will be training me."

Skye was glad she had not taken him up on his offer for refreshments, as she would have choked on them or spewed them all over the room at that moment. Jordan Turner wanted to get back into boxing? She thought as she looked at him, her features registering her shock.

"What? I thought when you walked away from competitive boxing, you swore to my father you would never fight again." She was still in a little bit of shock at the bombshell he had unloaded. "It upset my father when you walked away without a care as to how your sudden decision affected the rest of your boxing team. No explanation."

"A lot happened that year." Jordan's features changed. He looked haunted for a minute before gathering his composure and giving her a tight smile. "To be honest, that was not my finest hour or the best decision I ever made. It was made in the heat of an emotional moment." Standing, he ran his hand through his hair as if to compose himself before sitting back down. "Look, between you and me, I have regretted my decision nearly every single day since the dust of that year settled."

"And..." Skye's eyes narrowed on him as she asked, "now you think you can just step back into the boxing world where you left off? As if you never left?"

"Of course not," Jordan said with a small snort. "I am not that egotistical to think I could ever do that. I have been out of the sport for five years now."

"My father always thought you could be even greater than most of your heroes," Skye said passionately. "He had a great knack for spotting talent and an even better one for knowing who would make it." She gave him a sad smile. "I think you were one of the only times he was ever wrong about that."

"Ouch," Jordan grabbed his heart theatrically. "I guess I deserved that."

"You do. Now, what is all this really about?" Skye looked at Jordan quizzically. "You obviously don't need the money." Her brows drew together as she eyed him intently. "You have a very lucrative modeling career on all accounts. You cannot drive around the city without seeing your face plastered on some billboard. Plus, you have a fast-growing sporting line business." She tilted her head, biting her lower lip contemplatively. "So, is this about proving something? Did someone bruise your tender ego?" She gave him a smug smile.

"Again, ouch," Jordan said, leaning forward. "If you are

finished stabbing me with your well-aimed verbal daggers, maybe you will hear me out?"

"Sure," Skye shrugged. "That is what I came all this way for."

"I had my reasons for quitting five years ago," Jordan explained to Skye. "They are very personal reasons that I do not spread around the place."

"I know," Skye told him coolly, as her face was devoid of any expression. His dumping her father had almost ruined the business. "My father told me about your brother. My condolences, by the way. I know it's rather late, but you never really gave us a chance to say it back then when you left without a word or backward glance."

"I am going to overlook the barbed words in there and thank you for your condolences." Jordan sighed as he looked into her big caramel eyes. They were beautiful eyes. He shook his head. *You will not go there, Jordan!* He admonished himself.

"So, why now? Why after all this time?" Skye looked at him as she tilted her head to one side, staring at him like she was trying to see into his head.

"I have been thinking of getting back into the ring for three years." Jordan sighed again. "I don't know if you remember my manager. Quinton?"

Skye nodded at Jordan. How could she forget that idiot? Skye thought.

Quinton was the one who had walked into the gym and callously dumped the news of Jordan's immediate retirement on her father, then left without another word. Her father had had his first heart attack that night. The severity of the attack had caused significant damage to his heart. After that, it was only a matter of time before her father had another heart attack. His rare blood type had made a donor match nearly impossible, and they could not revive him after the second major heart attack.

"How could I ever forget your errand boy?" Skye could not help the venom that had crept into her voice. She didn't care.

"Quinton always managed to talk me out of returning to the ring," Jordan chose to ignore her scathing remark. "But, I turned thirty this year, and this may be my last shot. I need to give it all I can."

"Okay," Skye said thoughtfully. "Suppose I agreed to train you. Where do you see your comeback taking you in the boxing world?"

"You are just like your father." Jordan smiled as he thought about the start of his boxing career and meeting Vic Larsen for the first time.

Vic was a legend as far as boxing coaches went. Jordan had been thrilled that his father was able to convince Vic to give him a shot. He remembered Skye as a budding tween at the time. Her dark brown hair in ponytails, a spattering of freckles across her cute nose, ripped jeans, and skateboard in hand, she watched him from the sidelines. She was also always accompanied by her lanky blonde friend.

"I will take that as a compliment." Skye smiled at him.

"Whatever happened to your tall, skinny blonde friend?" Jordan asked her curiously. "The nerdy one that always had her nose in a book. She loved to point out the damage I was doing to my body."

"Carly is now Dr. Carly O'Brien," Skye said proudly. "She is an orthopedic surgeon and has specialized in sports medicine." Skye raised one eyebrow at Jordan. "If you ever meet her, and by reviving a boxing career at your age, the probability of that is high you will." She gave Jordan a smug smile at the look of surprise on his face. "Don't call her a nerd. She is licensed to wield huge needles and cut you open."

"Duly noted," Jordan said. "I believe you got your degree in sports sciences."

"I did," Skye said uneasily. She did not like talking about herself. "I also have a degree in sports management. Then all the other required certifications allow me to train and coach. But then you already know this!" She eyed him suspiciously.

"I do," Jordan said and nodded. "I admit to looking you up a while ago when I first decided I was going to give boxing another shot."

"It is going to be a lot of hard work," Skye told him, her eyes deliberately traveling over his torso. "You are not in the best shape for a boxer."

"You are not the first person to tell me that lately." Jordan laughed a little nervously, recalling the "dad bod" comparison.

When her eyes had traveled over Jordan's body, it had felt as if it were her hands. Jordan swallowed, fighting to control his wayward body and thoughts. Hopefully, Skye was going to be his coach. Mixing business with pleasure always ended in disaster, and he needed her training abilities. Nothing more.

"You do know that it is going to be hard work, and you would need to stick to my training routine," Skye told him. "I would also need to talk to anyone who cooks your meals, or I'll go over your eating plan with you."

"So, does this mean you will train me?" Jordan smiled, relieved.

"It means I am thinking about it," Skye told him. "Where do you plan to train?"

"Why don't I show you?" Jordan stood up. "I have my own personal gym, complete with a twenty-seven yard heated pool."

"Okay," Skye stood and followed Jordan to the back of the house.

Skye was not surprised when they stepped into a high-tech ultra-modern training room complete with a full-size boxing ring. Jordan stepped back to allow Skye to enter before them. As she did, her shoulder accidentally brushed against his arm, causing her heart to jolt. She put some distance between them.

"Impressive," Skye said as she looked around. She felt like a kid opening Christmas presents. "If I agree to this, you would need to be up early. You would also be training for a good portion of the day."

"I have done this before, Skye," Jordan said, watching her look around the gym. "I am fully prepared to do whatever it takes to get back into the game."

"Okay." Skye sighed. "I know I am probably going to regret this, but okay, I will do it."

"Thank you, Skye," Jordan said softly, moving to stand close to her. "You have no idea what this means to me."

"To be honest." Skye looked at him, her gaze cool and level. "The gym could use the publicity."

"Of course," Jordan agreed. "It will be quite the comeback story." He folded his arms in front of him to stop them from reaching out and hugging her. She did not like him being close to her.

"Fine," Skye agreed. "I will train you. But on my terms and with my training as well as my diet regimen."

"I will need you to stay here for the season." Jordan shocked her with his stipulation. "As I need to get up early and will train throughout the day, it is best to cut the back and forth travel for our itinerary."

"I have other clients, Jordan," Skye told him. "I can't be solely at your beck and call."

"I am willing to pay you three times your normal rate." Jordan proceeded to give her a payment proposal. "I am sure you have someone you can trust to run the gym without you for a while. You can then go to the gym when we are off our training schedule and on your days off."

"That is a hefty amount." Skye stared at him, shocked. "I

will need a day or two to get things organized. It will also give you a chance to rest up or get whatever restlessness you have in your soul out before we begin." She gave Jordan a tight smile. "My training regimen is no joke but is designed to give you the maximum benefit for optimal conditioning."

"Then I can expect you on Monday?" Jordan held out his hand. "Once again, thank you, Skye."

"Monday it is; please make sure I can talk to whoever makes your meals and your manager." Skye put on her most professional air.

"I will organize that for you," Jordan said as he walked with her through the house to her car and opened the door for her. "I do appreciate you doing this for me, Skye," he said softly.

"Let's see how much you appreciate me in a week?" she gave him an evil smile. "If you want to get into a few competitions this year, you have a lot of work to do."

Skye got into her car and drove off. Her mind reeled when the excitement of Jordan's offer flowed through her.

"Dad," Skye talked to the photo she had of him on her key ring. "I think I may be able to keep the doors to Vic's Gym open for a while longer and even bring in customers again."

Feeling elated, she turned on the radio and flipped through the stations until she found a song she could sing along to at the top of her lungs.

CHAPTER 4
The Larsen Way

"I THINK with those few changes to the app, we can probably push through with the agreed launch date," Jordan, who was sat back in his chair as head of the table in his company's ultra-modern boardroom, announced. "Paige, how are the new women's training pants?"

"The first few tests were not too great with the new material," Paige replied, pushing her glasses up her nose. "I have sent the results back to the factory for some enhancements. But we are a lot closer to making a more breathable, absorbent material than we were a month ago."

"Any chance we will be able to set a launch date for the early new year?" Jordan asked as he leaned forward on the table, looking at this company's lead designer for women's wear. "I would have ideally wanted to launch these new training pants for Christmas."

"I know," said Paige, giving Jordan a tight smile. "We are getting there; we want to knock the competition out of the running with our new material and design."

"I have every confidence you will, Paige." Jordan gave her

an encouraging smile. "Are there any other pressing matters before I leave?" He looked around the table at his team. "Paige knows how to get hold of me; please take pressing matters to her. As you know, I will be training for the next few weeks and will be holding our meetings on internet conference calls."

"We are happy that you have decided to get back in the ring," said Paige, smiling at Jordan. "We are all rooting for you."

Jordan's staff left the meeting while he stayed seated, going over some of the matters his team had discussed.

"I thought we were going to lunch?" Quinton asked, poking his head through the doorway.

"I just need to drop these papers off with Heather, my secretary who nearly quit because of you, remember?"

"Yeah." Quinton grinned cheekily. "The woman is beautiful but a little too needy for me. She basically wanted me to commit to a relationship on the first date."

"Quinton." Jordan shook his head at his friend. "You went out for nearly two years."

"Like I said," Quinton shrugged, "she wanted a commitment from me way too soon in our relationship."

"Funny how you have not been in a relationship since," Jordan remarked, his eyebrows raised at Quinton. "You have also avoided dating whenever you could since the breakup as well."

"You know me," Quinton said, smiling. "Just weighing up my options."

"Wait here," Jordan told him, shaking his head and sighing. "I will just drop these off with Heather and grab my golf clubs."

"I will make sure they have a table for us at the golf club." Quinton took out his phone and walked off to the elevator before adding, "I will meet you in the lobby."

"So Skye Larsen..." Quinton pressed the tee into the ground and positioned his golf ball. "I hear most of Vic's customers left the gym after he passed away, as they did not have much confidence in her abilities to run the gym or coach." He teed off perfectly.

"Well, I disagree with their ignorance," Jordan said, stepping up and getting ready to tee off. "I trained with her a few times when Vic was unable to coach me. She was Vic 2.0."

"Yeah," Quinton said, and they walked to where Quinton's golf ball had landed. "I remember Vic had a few heart problems last year." Quinton picked out the golf club he needed to play the shot. "I did not know it was Skye who had coached you on Vic's off days." He swung, connecting with the small ball and sending it flying.

"You never asked," Jordan said as he and Quinton walked to find Jordan's ball. "You did, however, comment on how well I had fought after each match that I had trained for with Skye."

"Ah," Quinton remarked, as he watched Jordan send the ball expertly onto the green. "I do remember those few matches. Your punches seemed cleaner, and your footwork a lot smoother."

"Correct," Jordan said, placing his golf club behind his shoulders while watching Quinton line up his next shot. "That was five years ago now. I believe she even trained Carter Barnes."

"Carter Barnes? No way." Quinton looked impressed. "He is my favorite MMA fighter of all time," Quinton added, wide-eyed. "Do you think she would introduce us? I have been trying to talk to him for years."

"Wow!" Jordan exclaimed and shook his head. "It took one name drop to get you on board with Skye as my coach."

"No," said Quinton, who had now stopped lining up his shot to look at Jordan. "You had me at 'Skye Larsen will be coaching me'. I know how awesome she is. I have seen it in the young talent she has been training. There is one kid, in particular, that she trained that I would love to manage."

"Hey," Jordan said, waving the back of his golf club at Quinton. "You need to be concentrating on your number one client right now, and that is me."

"Seriously?" Quinton laughed. "You don't have to be jelly, dude. You will always be my number one," he said, in his calm voice.

"Jelly?" Jordan gave Quinton a disgusted look. "Since when do you use words like jelly and dude?" He laughed, lining up his shot.

"Since I want to sign that kid at Skye's gym," Quinton said excitedly. "I'm telling you, Quint, he is the next Carter Barnes. He may even be better than Carter."

"So you are getting yourself back into the world of MMA?" Jordan smiled at his best friend. "I don't know why you ever quit participating in the sport?"

"If you remember, I have pins in my jaw from the sport, as well as a rebuilt knee, so..." Quinton chose another club. "I'm pretty much an old messed-up biddy now where that sport is concerned."

"Rubbish, and you know it," Jordan said and stood back as Quinton swung his golf club. "What happened in that cage fight was not your fault."

"Like what happened to Wayne was not yours?" Quinton turned around to face Jordan.

"Touché," Jordan said softly. "But the difference between Wayne's accident and that kid in the cage is that I had the power to stop Wayne from driving." They found Jordan's golf ball, and he chose his club as he continued to say, "You, on the other hand, did not know about the kid's heart condition. He should never have been in the ring in the first place." Jordan swung, sending his ball flying. "That is on the kid, his coach, physician, and father."

"Still, it was my fists that sent him to his grave," Quinton said sadly, his eyes haunted with the memory of that day. "Anyway, I am way too old to get back into that sport now. Besides, it has been almost ten years for me, but only five for you."

"Yeah," Jordan said, leaning on his club and giving his friend the once over. "And getting you back in shape would be a mammoth task." He laughed and duck as a tee was aimed at his head.

"But seriously, Jordan..." Quinton packed away his clubs as they got ready to play the last hole. "You fight in six weeks; do you think you will be ready then?"

"I've done it before," Jordan said with confidence. "With Skye's new training regime, I am sure it will be possible."

"Yeah." Quinton gave a guffaw. "I have seen her exercise regime, and I must say my condolences to you now. I think you are barely going to be able to feel your extremities after each session."

"I spoke to Bennie," Jordan said as he swung his last shot. "That kid you want to take on as a client. He helped her with her new training regimen. He reckons that his win rate has gone up since he started it. Even your hero Carter Barnes swears by it that Skye trains his son."

Quinton whistled. "Carter Barnes' son is training for MMA?" He looked a little surprised. "I know Carter quit the MMA because of his late wife, so I didn't think he would let his son to engage in the sport."

"I believe young Barnes is a boxer, not an MMA fighter," Jordan informed him as he putted his ball into the hole. "And once again, I have crushed you in a round of golf." Jordan gave Quinton a big smile.

"You know I only let you win because you are not only my

best friend but also a client," Quinton defended his loss. "It is the rules of golf."

"Sure, buddy." Jordan laughed as they collected their golf bags and walked back to the club. "I hope they have a table for us now as I am starved, having missed lunch."

"They gave us a snack for giving away our table," Quinton defended his favorite golf club. "The lovely maître d' is doing the best she can; their restaurant is trendy."

"We both know the reason you love to play golf and eat at this club has nothing to do with their greens or food," Jordan sighed as they entered the changing rooms and got ready to go eat.

"That is quite a tight boxing schedule," Jordan said as he looked over the itinerary Quinton had handed him while they ate their late lunch. "If I cannot get back into the top league, I have to do five to seven fights with three-week intervals in between each fight?"

"Well," Quinton said, cutting into his tender, perfectly cooked steak, "I am going to try and convince the committee to let you do three entry-level fights to qualify for more championship fights."

"So, my boxing comeback is now in the hands of the boxing committee," Jordan said, letting the document flutter onto the table. "As long as they get me to where I need to be, I am sure I will cope."

"I still think you are nuts," Quinton replied, taking another bite of his steak. "But I am sure you will do as well as you always do. Especially with your drive to succeed in everything you do."

"Here's to coming out of retirement." Jordan raised his glass of wine with Quinton.

"Here's to a whole new collection of wins for you, my friend," Quinton toasted.

Jordan was up early on the Monday morning that Skye was to arrive. He was showered and dressed before six. He pottered around in the gym, making sure everything was in place. He had checked his boxing gear a few times and kept checking the time.

Jordan had knots in his stomach, and his nerves were on edge. What the hell was wrong with him? Why was he feeling so anxious? He even caught himself watching the driveway from the window, waiting for Skye to arrive. Time had all but slowed down as it ticked at a snail's pace to eight o'clock.

Jordan's heart skipped a beat when he saw her car pulling into the driveway at eight o'clock sharp. Slow down, boy! Jordan had to keep himself from rushing to the front door like an overly eager puppy. Hell, he had never been this nervous about anything in his life!

Hearing the doorbell ring, Jordan waited for a few beats before calling out to his housekeeper that he would get it.

"Good morning. As prompt as always," Jordan greeted her with a smile. His throat went dry, and his heart jolted when he looked at her.

"Hey." Skye smiled back. "Do you think you could give me a hand with my luggage?"

Jordan stood staring at her, taking in her petite frame seductively outlined by her training clothes. He swallowed hard, trying to wet his throat so his voice would not give away the effect she was having on him with her cute smile, buoyant ponytail, and well-toned figure.

"Too much?" she asked him, frowning.

"What?" Jordan looked at her questioningly, hoping his face hadn't given him away.

"My luggage," Skye clarified. "Is it too much?"

"Oh." Jordan shook his head. Snap out of it, idiot; she is your coach. "Not at all." He smiled. "I will get us some help."

Jordan called his gardener to come and help them take Skye's luggage to her room.

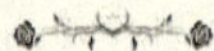

"Quinton gave me the fights he has set up for you," Skye told Jordan as they sat going over his training program. "I think the first fight in six weeks is ambitious. But your saving grace is that you have kept up with a physical fitness regime."

"Thank you for your confidence in me," Jordan said with a smile. "You are the first one to say that to me; everyone else tells me how out of shape I am."

"I am sure they meant out of shape for boxing," Skye told him earnestly. "You are by no means out of shape physically." She immediately regretted her words, and her cheeks flamed.

"Can you say that for me again so I can record it and play it for Quinton?" Jordan laughed, feeling elated that she had noticed him that way! *Stop it, Jordan!* He admonished himself. She is your coach, and you want to get back into boxing; you are not going there!

"I am sure he is merely ragging on you," Skye said and cleared her throat. "I think we can start with some light sparring today so I can see what we need to work on. I hope you don't mind, but I asked my young trainer Joey to join us today." She looked at her watch. "He should be here any minute."

"Not at all." Jordan sat back, placing his foot on his knee. "Is Joey the young MMA fighter I have heard so much about?"

"Yes, he is," Skye answered, looking at Jordan curiously. "Who told you about Joey?"

"Quinton." Jordan raised his eyebrows, smiling at the look of ahhh Skye got on her face. "He thinks the kid has great potential."

"Wasn't Quinton an upcoming MMA fighter once?" Skye asked Jordan.

"Yes," Jordan confirmed. "He stopped fighting a few months before his twenty-first birthday. He has a few bothersome injuries from fighting."

"So, now he is looking into managing MMA fighters?" Skye asked.

"It looks that way." Jordan told her about the conversation he had with Quinton about wanting to manage Joey.

"I guess I could speak to Joey," Skye said. "Bennie has been his informal manager."

"I know; I spoke to Bennie a few days ago when I called the gym looking for you." Jordan smiled fondly as he remembered their conversation. "He is the same old Bennie."

"You cannot find a better person than Bennie." Skye's features softened and changed when she mentioned him. "He is my second father."

"I know that too," Jordan said, his eyes wide opened. "I was warned with my life not to let you down in any way." He laughed as her cheeks went red again in embarrassment.

"Yes," Skye said, a little mortified. "He can be quite protective."

The bell rang, interrupting them.

"That must be Joey," said Skye, feeling relieved. Her cheeks felt like they were on fire.

"So that kid is seriously fast," Jordan said as he wiped the perspiration from his brow. "I can see why Quinton is so interested in him now."

"He is fast, and his footwork is impeccable." Skye smiled as she watched Joey ooh and aah over Jordan's fully equipped gym. "Which is more than I can say for yours right now."

"Thanks." Jordan looked a little taken aback at first. "You are right, though. My footwork got sloppy trying to compensate for Joey's speed. He's exceptional."

"I know you two are not well matched weight-wise," Skye explained to Jordan. "But Joey is nimble and quick. I would like you to work with him a few times a week as I believe he is the key to increasing your speed and tightening up your footwork."

"Would you object to my watching a few of those training sessions?" Quinton asked from the entrance of the gym.

"Hello, Quinton." Skye's shoulders stiffened, and her demeanor cooled down. She did her best to put on a neutral face.

"How are you, Skye?" Quinton smiled warmly at her, a little confused over her frosty reception.

"I am well," Skye replied with a tight smile. "If Jordan has no objection, then it is fine by me." "Will you excuse me? She asked, nodding, "I need to go and discuss the sparring sessions with Joey."

"Good to see you again." Quinton nodded back as she turned and walked to where Joey was practicing his moves on one of the heavyweight punching bags hung up in the training room.

"Was it something I said?" Quinton asked Jordan, his brows drawn together as he watched Skye advise Joey on some of the moves he was practicing. "So, I see you have met my potential new MMA client?"

"I can see why you would want to drive his career," Jordan

said, pulling off his sweat-stained shirt while heading to the locker room with Quinton hot on his heels. "The kid is really fast and has excellent instincts. It is like he can feel a person's next move."

"Yeah." Quinton nodded. "I watched his last fight. His opponent had no chance. The kid countered nearly every one of his opponent's moves."

"Skye told me that Joey's father left them when he was young, and his mother raised him and his three siblings." Jordan pulled on a fresh shirt. "He started fighting as a means to help supplement his mother's income. Vic found the kid at a fight where he was totally outmatched but was able to take down his opponent."

"Oh, wow!" Quinton looked impressed. "I take it the fight Vic found him at was an off-the-book one?"

"Uh-huh," Jordan said as he reached for a clean towel. "Vic put Joey in Skye's care, and with the help of your boy crush Carter Barnes, they were able to mold him into an upcoming MMA fighter."

"That kind of story sells fighters even more," Quinton said, his eyes were filled with the excitement of possibilities for Joey's career. "I knew this kid was going to be a star."

"Uh..." Jordan said, pointing to himself. "Remember, right now, I am your number one priority."

"Yeah, yeah," Quinton said, absently-mindedly. "But you still have six weeks and are already set up. I have gone over all the media for the fights, bookings, blah, blah, blah." Quinton said, grinning. "So that frees up some time for me to get the kid to come around to me being his new manager."

"Good luck with that," Jordan remarked and walked past Quinton to the back of the gym. "You have to get through his coach and Bennie first. Oh, and did I mention Skye said that Carter Barnes had agreed to help coach Joey too?"

"WHAT?" Quinton choked on his saliva. This was like

receiving presents on Christmas. "Oh, my word! This just gets better and better."

"Well," Jordan said, tilting his head in Skye's direction. "You will have to get into her good graces first, as Joey is very loyal to her and Vic's Gym."

"Yeah." Quinton nodded, his eyes narrowing while he looked at Skye. "You are right. She was kind of frosty towards me." He looked at Jordan, his face splitting into a smile. "I will have to win her over with my incredible charm."

"I am warning you, Quint," Jordan said seriously, as his voice held a serious threat. "Don't do anything to jeopardize this opportunity for me. Anything."

"No," Quinton said, frowning at Jordan, looking a little hurt. "I would never do that. I know you are going to use Heather as exhibit A. Still, she was an exception to 'my don't date members of the Jordan entourage' policy."

"Glad to hear it," Jordan said and grabbed a bottle of water off the counter. "I will hold you to that."

"Well, now that that is out of the way, why don't you invite me to dinner and suggest the kid stay as well?" Quinton gave Jordan a big grin. "That way, I get to charm Skye and drop hints that the kid needs a serious manager—me!"

"You know no shame," Jordan said, shaking his head.

Quinton chuckled. "No, I don't."

CHAPTER 5

Falling Into a New Routine

Skye's alarm screamed at her from the nightstand next to the large bed. She woke in the room that was to be her home for the next six weeks or so. Her hand reached out and grabbed her phone. She pressed the screen, turning off the shrill noise. She had had hardly any sleep. She would dearly love to blame it on an over-excited Joey from Quinton's interest in his career and the fact she had slept in a strange house in a strange bed. But if the truth were told, her restless night had more to do with the owner of the house.

Jordan was even more gorgeous up close and personal than she had remembered. His face, voice, the smell of his cologne, all tormented her through the night. She had to set the ground rules, and that was NO DATING OR FANTASIZING about Jordan. She gave herself a mental lecture.

Skye went about her morning wake-up routine. It involved a shower, brushing her teeth, applying face cream, scraping her unruly thick hair into a ponytail, and getting dressed. Her usual attire was either training tights or sweatpants and a t-shirt or gym shirt. That morning, it was tights and a gym shirt with her favorite pair of running shoes. Skye and Jordan needed to start the morning off with a new running routine.

But first, she had to go hunt down Jordan's personal chef, which, of course he has, and make sure he was ready to prepare the diet Skye had laid out for Jordan. Skye liked Malcolm, Jordan's chef; he was friendly and seemed excited to get her diet plan. He did not even flinch when Jordan had him sign all the non-disclosure forms. Wow, Dad had a lot of rules for his household staff. Even poor Joey had to sign a million documents before he could spar with Jordan yesterday.

Skye shook off the fluttering in her stomach; she had to get a grip on her girlie crush. She was a professional trainer now and needed to focus on getting her boxer ready for his first fight. That meant no distractions or wayward feelings getting in the way.

Why the heck does one man need such a big house? Skye wondered as she padded into the kitchen. There were only so many rooms one could use at once! Here Skye was, thinking her three-bedroom apartment was too big for one person.

She was so deep in thought that she didn't see Jordan until it was too late, and she walked right into him.

"Sorry, I was not looking where I was...." Skye swallowed, trying to lubricate her suddenly dry throat. Her gaze was drawn to his ripped naked torso and traveled up to connect with his amber eyes.

"Good morning to you," Jordan said, smiling down at her. "For a moment there, I thought I had almost knocked down a smurf." He laughed as her cheeks colored. "The color of your training outfit makes your eyes a nice shade of honey."

"So, now I'm a Smurf with chameleon eyes!" Skye laughed, taking a few steps back to create some space between herself and his naked upper body. "Are you ready to start training?" she asked, taking her mind off his body.

"Yes," Jordan replied, saluting her. "I will quickly go grab my shirt, and we will get running." He stepped around Skye and headed out of the kitchen, saying. "Will you grab the bottles of water I put on the counter, please?"

"Sure." Skye picked up the two icy bottles of water. "Aren't there any at room temperature?" She looked around the kitchen; she did not like drinking such cold water when she trained.

"Here you go," Malcolm said as he entered the kitchen as silently as a cat, making Skye jump.

"Thank you." Skye smiled at him. "We'll be back in roughly an hour."

"No problem. I will have the healthy oats with berries, nuts, and everything you ordered already," Malcolm said, smiling at her. "I am going to enjoy working with you over the next month or so."

"Thank you, Malcolm." Skye started walking to the door but stopped to say, "You should go and speak to Alyssa at the diner I told you about. I know she is looking to expand their business now."

"I did send her a message last night," Malcolm told her excitedly. "We have a meeting on Wednesday. Thank you, Skye."

"No, thank you. You're the one who has to do the hard work." she smiled. "See you in an hour."

"We start with a one-mile warm-up after we have finished stretching." Skye demonstrated the first stretching routine Jordan needed to learn. "Don't dip too low and pull your muscles too much. You want to loosen them without tearing them, or it will knock your training back." Skye stood up, pulling her foot up towards her bottom.

Jordan did the same, only he wobbled a bit before finding his balance.

"The trick to finding your balance is to focus on a point, like a spot on a tree or something stable," Skye explained. "Feel yourself anchored to the ground; don't take your eyes off the object, then slowly lift your foot."

Jordan nodded, his blue eyes fixed on her green ones. A slow, sexy smile spread across his face as he lifted his foot to his butt without a wobble.

"You're right," he said, his voice soft and seductive. "Focusing on a point does center you."

Skye's heart seemed to stop for a second. Her breath caught in her throat, the tip of her tongue darted out to lick her dry lips. She blinked stupidly when her watch bleeped. Clearing her throat, she quickly looked away to shake out her legs and arms.

"Well done," Skye gave Jordan a tight smile. "So, one mile at a steady pace," she ordered and took off with Jordan close behind her.

This was going to be a lot harder than Skye thought it would be; the man was just too sexy for his own darn good.

"Okay," Jordan said as he drank his second bottle of water. "I can feel how intense that workout method was." He frowned at Skye. "But I thought we were running at least five miles."

"Not today," Skye's said, her eyes narrowing as she fiddled with her oats. "Today, we start your program from scratch. You can't just go jumping into training in the middle of the program."

"I'm already physically fit and run a good five to seven

miles a day," Jordan argued. "Now you also tell me I am not going to spar today?" His eyes narrowed.

"You are a retired boxer," Skye said, shaking her head. "You know that you don't spar every day."

"Yes, but you are still assessing my technique," said Jordan, taking a spoonful of his oats and looking down at his training program that Skye had printed out for him. "Swimming before lunch?"

"Swimming helps increase your cardio and endurance without putting a strain on your joints," Skye explained to him. "You don't want to incur injuries before you have gotten back into the ring." She eyed him out. "If you listen to me, you will be able to build up strength in that shoulder you seem to favor." She gave him a smug smile at his astonished look.

"I should have known you would notice that." Jordan's mouth lifted in a half-smile. "You are as sharp as your father."

"I'm sure any fighter worthy of their salt will be able to pick up on that too," Skye responded, raising her eyebrows at him. "You try to cover it up by leading with your left when you are right-handed. Your opponent, or at least his trainer, will notice that, and they will use it against you."

"I guess my right shoulder has become a bit lazy," Jordan said as he automatically rotated his right shoulder, trying his best not to flinch from the little pinch he felt in it.

"That first punch you landed yesterday wasn't because Joey was slow or unprepared," Skye said as she narrowed her eyes. "It was so he could assess your weaknesses and the strength of your punch."

"You let me almost knock the kid out to assess my weakness," Jordan whistled. "You are brutal." He mocked her.

"Oh, you would never have knocked Joey out, and you barely tapped him," Skye assured Jordan. "He is way too fast for that."

"Okay, well, that was a little hurtful and bruising to my

ego." Jordan snorted. "He is also smaller, lighter, and a lot younger than me," he said, defensively. "I wasn't going to throw my hardest punch at him."

"Your left side is not your powerhouse side," Skye told Jordan. "And if you can catch Joey, imagine what you can do in the ring with a bigger, heavier opponent in your weight class."

"Ah," Jordan said, finally catching on to Skye's way of thinking. "He is going to help me with my speed and technique."

"Correct," Skye said and nodded. "Joey started boxing but fell in love with MMA. I think he still sneaks off to underground cage fights. I have seen him cover up quite a few split lips and bruises in the past."

"To be young and fearless," Jordan breathed. "I hope you nipped that in the bud, as those fights can not only get Joey seriously injured but killed."

"I know." Skye shook her head. "It took Carter and Bennie to threaten him with his life to stop him from those fights. But I think he was doing it for the money, to help his mom."

"That is so sad." Jordan shook his head. "Maybe I could help him out by giving him some chores around my office or gym?"

"That is very sweet," Skye said, impressed and surprised by Jordan's genuine concern. "But Carter and Bennie have got together to get him some sponsors. I think they are both secretly his biggest sponsors right now, but at least it stops Joey from trolling those illegal clubs."

"If he got caught, it would also end his career before it began," Jordan said with concern.

"I know." Skye sighed. "But there is not much a person can do to keep food on the table and a roof over their heads." She smiled sadly.

"I see you have scheduled three sparring sessions a week,"

Jordan said, turning the training session pages. "You have Joey sparring with me twice a week on alternate weeks and once a week in between." He looked at her, questioningly. "Who is the second sparring partner?"

"None other than Carter Barnes." Skye gave Jordan a smug smile at his shocked look.

"That is not fair," Jordan breathed. "Both of my sparring partners do mix martial arts."

"Uh-huh," Skye picked up the steaming cup of coffee Malcolm had just poured for her. "They are also fully trained boxers." She looked at him, grinning. "Carter is your fighting weight. He is fast and powerful. He is also trained to judge his opponent's next move on a reflex. Sparring with him will help you do the same and throw more accurate punches."

"I thought maybe Bennie—" Jordan said, looking a little pale at the thought of sparring with the great Carter Barnes. "He is more in my league."

"You are funny." Skye stopped Jordan from adding cream to his coffee. "Yeah, no more fluff in your java. It is black and sugar-free from now on." She laughed at his pained look. "And for the record, Bennie would probably knock you on your butt in a real fight. He is in great shape." She deliberately let her eyes run pointedly over Jordan's body.

"Ouch," Jordan grabbed his chest dramatically. "I get the point. I have a lot of work to do, and no more cream and sugar to make my life easier."

"Visualize the end result," Skye said, as she laughed at his pained expression. "Only you have the power to move yourself to where you want to be."

"Where have I heard that before?" Jordan rolled his eyes. "Remember when I told you, you were just like your father. I was wrong. I can see now his training sessions were like summer camp compared to your military-style boot camp." He picked up the training itinerary.

"If it's too much, you could always go back into retirement?" She smiled sweetly at him before getting ready to leave the breakfast table. "You have two hours to attend your meetings and get ready for the next session. Malcolm will bring you your light snack an hour before."

"Yes, sir." Jordan saluted her again. "What are you going to do with your next two hours?" He neatened the papers in his hands, trying not to look too interested. "Call the boyfriend to let him know you are okay?" He looked up and smiled candidly.

"No," Skye said, skirting around the hint to find out if she was seeing someone. Best if he was not sure if she was in a relationship or not, Skye reasoned. "I need to call Bennie and Joey to make sure everything is okay at the gym. I also have to make some appointments with Carly for a few of my customers."

"Oh, right," said Jordan, looked at Skye questioningly. "You mentioned that she is into sports medicine."

"Yes." Skye's eyes looked pointedly at Jordan's right shoulder. "I would like her to take a look at your right shoulder to make sure it is okay."

"Nah," Jordan flexed his shoulder again. "It's good. I think I just overdid my gym session last Friday."

"Okay." Skye took the hint. He did not want to discuss his shoulder. "But don't do any off-schedule training from today onwards. Your old training regimen stops as of today. Mine begins now."

"Of course," Jordan said as he stood up, staring down at her. "My training regime is entirely in your hands from this point on."

Skye left the kitchen, thinking that she would need to keep a close eye on his shoulder. She knew it could become problematic, as she was sure it was a little more painful than Jordan was letting on.

CHAPTER 6

Amazing Results

Jordan's routine had been established, and he was settling into Skye's method of training. He had to admit that he was already seeing and feeling an improvement after only five days. Jordan was impressed and a little ticked off with those members and staff of Vic's Gym that had left because they did not believe she had what it took to be a coach, let alone run a gym.

During their earlier mid-morning session, Skye got into the ring to demonstrate how he could improve his right arm swing. Jordan knew she saw that his shoulder was a bit bothersome, but she never pushed him about it. She gave him workouts and routines that did not put a lot of pressure on the joints. While Skye was in the ring with him, she also showed him how to protect his right shoulder, which she now called his lazy arm.

Jordan knew Skye had every reason to be concerned about his shoulder, and he also knew he should get it checked out. But Jordan only had a set amount of time to get ready before his first fight. It was bad enough that he may have to start in a lower league because the boxing committee thought he had been out of boxing for too long now. Quinton was meeting with them at the moment to find out which fights Jordan would be participating in. The one Quinton had initially booked was pending the outcome of his meeting with the committee.

Jordan sighed. Coming out of boxing retirement turned out to be a little more complicated than he thought it would be. Jordan looked at his watch and picked up his laptop; it was almost time for his online conference call to the office. Before he hit the button to dial in, Malcolm entered carrying a tray.

"Your snack, as requested by Skye," Malcolm said as he set the tray down. "Try those homemade protein bars; they are to die for," he added, impressed. "That Skye is amazing." His eyes lit up as he mentioned her.

Something twitched in Jordan's chest as Malcolm looked a little star-struck by Skye. Was he feeling a little green? he wondered. That was ridiculous; Malcolm and Skye had only just met, and she was helping him create Jordan's diet. But still, he felt a little jealous of the time Malcolm got to spend with her. Cut it out, Jordan! He gave himself a little lecture about mixing training and pleasure. He had to keep his mind on the fight.

"Did you hear a word I was saying?" Malcolm looked at him through his narrowed eyes. "You have been staring off into space while I ran crocodile flesh mixed with snake liver past you."

"What? Sorry," Jordan shook his head, then looked at Malcolm, amused. "Did I just agree to add those ingredients to my menu?"

"Yeah," Malcolm replied, looking down at Jordan questioningly. "You did so without blinking too."

"I have a lot on my mind with coming out of retirement and launching this new line." Jordan picked up a homemade protein bar and bit into it. His mouth salivated. "Oh wow!" he exclaimed, taking another bite. "These are good. Where did she get the recipe from?"

"Can you believe it is one of her own recipes?" Malcolm nodded at Jordan's surprised look. "I am sure I gaped at Skye the same way you are gaping now when she told me. Turns out she is almost finished doing a Ph.D. in nutrition and dietetics."

"She never said anything about that," Jordan said as he picked up another bite-sized bar. "These are good. I wonder if she would be willing to market them. They'd sell."

"I don't think so," Malcolm said, shaking his head. "I already asked, and she said that maybe once she perfected them. But, as far as I am concerned, they don't get more perfect than they already are. So I took her answer as a polite no."

"Her whole nutritional plan should be marketed as far as I'm concerned," Jordan said. "Even though I am eating five to six small portions a day, I am eating half of what I used to and feel more energized and full."

"She is amazing." Malcolm sighed. "Promise me if you get her to market her program, you will let me do the meal side."

"Deal," Jordan said while noticing it was time for his meeting. "I am going to have to go into a meeting now. We will continue with this conversation later."

"I will hold you to that." Malcolm nodded and left the room.

"Hi, Paige," Jordan said into his headphones. "What updates do you have for me?"

"We have made some breakthroughs in the new material for the women's workout line," Paige informed him. "It is very exciting, and the test results should be out within a week."

"That is good news," Jordan breathed a sigh of relief. "It really is. I had a dreadful feeling we would be held up with that for months. How is the clothing design for the line coming along?"

"Well, we can have a few designs that I will send you in an hour." Paige did not look too thrilled. "But I am not sure if it is what we are looking for. I think they are too much like everything else out there."

"I trust your judgment, Paige," Jordan told her. "I will check them out later and get back to you with my two cents. But it is better to get a woman's opinion on this line. After all, women will be wearing them."

"Speaking of women," Paige smiled. "How is the training coming along? My husband tells me your new coach is a marvel, and he cannot stop talking about her. Should I be worried? He has even changed my diet," she groaned.

"I am sure he is breaking some clause in his contract with that," Jordan said, playfully. "Malcolm is right, though. At first, I thought that her approach was a bit new-age and would never work." He laughed. "I have been proven wrong. It has only been five days, and my stamina has increased, and I feel better than I ever have."

"Okay." Paige laughed. "Tell my husband that I will allow him to continue being a chef, as I too want to feel like that."

"I think everyone can benefit from a diet and fitness routine that Skye can provide," Jordan said thoughtfully.

"Do I see the wheels in your head turning?" Paige shook her head. "Let me guess, you are thinking of expanding into the food and fitness side now?"

"Oh, Paige," Jordan grinned at her. "You know me so well."

"That's because I'm your sister," Paige reminded him. "I know all your skeletons and where you have them buried." She laughed.

"I have to get to my afternoon session; I have to spar with Carter Barnes today," Jordan grinned while he name-dropped. "So, I guess I should expect to see Quinton any minute now."

"Oh wow," Paige said in awe. "Can I come too? He is still as hunky as ever. Do you remember I had a poster of him on my wall?"

"Yes, you and your crush on the guy," Jordan laughed. "Didn't you go to school with him?"

"I did, but he was two years ahead of me." Paige sighed. "Well, I had better head off to the labs. I will pop in tomorrow and bring you a piece of the material sample."

"Thanks, Paige," Jordan said and signed off the call.

"Were you talking about me?" Quinton frightened Jordan. He leaned against the door of the study with a big plate of food in his hands. "I heard you tell Paige that Carter was coming here today. What a bit of luck for me to have to pop in here to give your schedule and then discuss the outcome of the committee meeting with you," he said, innocently.

"Uh-huh," Jordan raised his eyebrows at Quinton. "You could have just told me over the phone." He laughed at his friend. "Well, are you going to stand there, eating all my food, or tell me what is going on with my new boxing career?" Jordan said impatiently, closing his laptop.

"It's just like we thought. The commission thinks you have been out of the game for too long to enter at the level we wanted to enter you at." Quinton took a bite of the dessert he was eating. "Have you tasted this tiramisu?" He pointed to the dish. "Malcolm is a gold mine of a chef. Your sister is so lucky to have married him."

"Yeah, I can remember you being completely heartbroken when Paige married another man," Jordan said, a half-smile on his face. "I often wondered if you were only friends with me to get to know her."

"Ouch." Quinton held his heart. "That was only partly true. Hanging out with the brother of the head cheerleader had its perks. But buddy, it has always been you and me." He laughed. "Okay, getting back to your boxing career revival. You are going to have to enter the seven fights I have listed for you. That's four fights to get back into the top league, and then three fights once you're there."

"So, by next year, I should be back in the top league?" Jordan looked at the amended fight schedule Quinton had put in front of him. "This is a heavy load, Quint." He frowned at his friend. "You know we will have to discuss it with Skye."

"Skye." Quinton sighed with starry eyes. "She is one mighty hot number wrapped up in a cute, petite package." He took another bite of the desert. "Do you know if she is seeing anyone?"

"Quint." Jordan leaned forward, his eyes boring into Quinton's. "You listen to me very carefully. Skye is off-limits to you; is that clear? Nearly losing me the best assistant I have ever had is one thing; I will not stand for you driving away my coach," he hissed.

"Okay, okay." Quinton looked taken aback. "Geez, I get it." He stood up, taking the fight schedule. "I will go discuss your itinerary with her." He walked to the door, saying, "Want to come to make sure I keep it all above board, sir?" His voice dripped with sarcasm.

"Seriously, Quint." Jordan got up, deciding he would go with Quinton.

Jordan knew his friend well, and Jordan may have inadvertently made Skye his next big challenge. Just thinking of Quinton leering after her made Jordan see red. He had to get a grip on himself. He and Skye could never have anything more than a professional relationship. Well, at least while she was his coach.

"This is a tough lineup, Quinton," Skye said, looking over the fight schedule and frowning. "Jordan needs at least three to four weeks between fights to recover."

"The first four fights of eight rounds of three minutes each," Quinton explained to Skye. "The only way Jordan is going to get back into the big league is if he works his way back up the ladder," he added, shaking his head.

"Why is the committee being so hard about this?" Skye looked at Quinton with her brows drawn. "Jordan was at the top of his game, undefeated, and a champion with three big win title belts to his name. That in itself should say enough."

"It's just the committee's way," Quinton shrugged, running his hand over his hair nervously. "If Jordan wants to get back to where he left off, this is the path he's going to have to take."

"At Jordan's age, he cannot afford to have more than five fights a year at the most," Skye said heatedly. "Now you are pushing it to six or seven?" She shoved the schedule back into Quinton's hands. "I think you are setting him up for a major fall. I do." She said, with concern giving her voice an edge.

"I know that this is a tight schedule," Quinton said, looking down at her as she held out the piece of paper. "But this is the only way he is going to fight his way back to the top," he said, exasperated.

"I want to go down on record by saying I think this is a bad idea," Skye said, pointing to the schedule. "I will do my best to keep him in top form between fights so that he sustains as few injuries as possible." Her green eyes blazed. "But if anything happens to him during one of these fights..." She raised her eyebrows. "That is on you." Skye turned away to greet Carter as he walked into the gym.

"Nice place," Carter chimed in, looking around the gym and giving a low whistle. "Here I thought my little room in the garage was the greatest training room." He grinned as he greeted Skye. "So, where is the ex-champ?"

"You guys and your sports crushes." Skye shook her head. She felt like a munchkin around the six-foot-three to six-foot-four giant men filling the room around her. "Carter, I would like you to meet Jordan Turner and his manager, Quinton Dickson."

"Quinton Dickson?" Carter greeted Jordan, then turned to Quinton, his brow creasing as he mulled over Quinton's name. "The same MMA junior champ, Quinton Dickson?"

"That would be me," Quinton grinned sheepishly as he extended his hand to greet his all-time idol. "I was two years behind you at the same high school."

"Yes," Carter recalled. "I think I read that. I was thrilled to know our school had produced such fighting champs as Jordan and you."

"I believe your son is training at Skye's gym," Jordan said.

"Yes," Carter smiled, putting down his gym bag. "He is boxing because I promised his mother I would never let him get into MMA."

"MMA is probably a lot safer than boxing when it comes to injuries," Skye chipped in, smiling as all eyes fell on her. "What?" She looked up at them. "It's true. Around seven to eight percent of boxers, at one point in their career, will lose consciousness and suffer serious injuries to the head, eyes, and many broken bones, especially in the facial area."

"She is right," Carter backed Skye up. "Most of the blood you see flying around a cage fight in MMA is from small cuts or bloody noses. MMA fighters also tend to have much longer careers than most boxers," he added, looking pointedly at Jordan and grinning.

"Good to know," Quinton said, nodding. "When you are done, do you think we could discuss that kid that works for

Skye, Joey?" he asked Carter. "I would love to be his manager and push his career. The kid is good."

"He is," Carter agreed. "But you would have to go over all this with Skye and Bennie first. They have only recently agreed to let me coach him. They are where his loyalty is."

"I will most definitely do that," Quinton said, pulling out his business card from his pocket. "I will give you this and then leave you to whip my friend over there into shape. I have a dinner date with my mother."

CHAPTER 7
It's Not a Date-Date

Skye was elated that Bennie had managed to get the bills sorted out with the weekly payments she had received from Jordan over the last three weeks. Bennie, Joey, and she were talking about the upcoming months for the gym. Carter had offered to help out while Skye was off training Jordan, and both Carter and Joey seemed grateful for his help.

"Jordan is happy to have his name associated with the gym, which may help bring in more business," Skye marked off the points to be discussed with the team. "I think that's it for now. If you need anything, give me a call."

"We will. Joey has rushed off, but he will be over this afternoon for a sparring session," Bennie said, as he ended the call.

Skye sat down to go over her budgets on her spreadsheet. A few more weeks like this and her finances may go from the red to the black. She breathed a small sigh of relief and smiled. She may be able to save the gym yet, pay her staff their full wages, and put some food on her table for a change.

She closed her laptop. It was time to go find Jordan for their morning training session. She padded through to his office. He was on a business call, so she stood at the door, pointing at her watch. He indicated that she should give him five more minutes, and then called her into the office when he was done.

"Maybe you can give us your opinion as a professional sportswoman on our new clothing line." Jordan picked up his laptop and moved to his office's lounge area so Skye could join him on the sofa. "Paige, this is Skye," he introduced Skye.

"Hi, I hear you're the one to thank for whipping my little brother into shape," Paige joked as Jordan grimaced. "As someone who I would think spends a lot of time in gym clothes, what would your perfect pair of sweatpants be?"

"Can I have a look at some of the designs?" Skye said. "Jordan has shown me the new material for your clothing line. I must admit it's amazing."

"Thank you. It has taken us nearly three years to perfect the material," Paige said proudly. "Now all we have to do is match the material to a design that is as unique as the new fabric."

Jordan handed her samples, and Skye sat down to discuss a few different designs that she felt would give a freer range of motion and be more comfortable while cutting down on chafe.

"Larger women would appreciate it," she mentioned as she rubbed the material between her fingers.

"Thank you, Skye," Paige said, impressed. "My husband and brother were right; you are a woman of many remarkable talents."

"Husband?" she cocked her head, frowning. "Do I know your husband?"

"Ah." Paige laughed on the other side of the screen. "I see no one there has told you. Malcolm is my other half."

"Oh; so you're the 'most amazing woman in the world' he

talks about all the time," Skye said and gave a little laugh. "I am so sorry; I did not connect you as *that* Paige."

"That is quite alright," Paige smiled. "I will be there this Sunday for a family meal, which I hope you will be joining us for. Don't worry; it will all be cooked to your instructions for Jordan."

"I never doubted that for a second." Skye smiled back. Paige was so easy to get along with. "I wouldn't want to impose on a family day."

"You won't be," Paige said. "It would be great to finally meet you in person, and besides, Quinton will be there too."

"Actually," Jordan said, leaning forward, "Sunday is Skye's day off, and I am sure she has better things to do than mingle with us."

"I am sure I can make it for lunch," Skye accepted Paige's offer. "Thank you, and Jordan, my day off is the next Sunday."

"Really?" Jordan frowned. "You are right," he said, after checking his calendar.

Paige said her goodbyes, and the call was disconnected.

"I think we are overdue to hit the gym," Skye gave Jordan a tight smile. "I bet Joey is already there and probably making use of all your equipment."

"Let the kid know he is more than welcome to train there whenever he likes, as long as it does not interfere with our sessions." Jordan followed Skye into the gym.

"You need to get your shoulder looked at," Skye said as she massaged Jordan's shoulder. "I think you should rest and ice it for the remainder of the day."

"It is fine," Jordan stressed as he flexed his arm once Skye had finished rubbing cream onto it. "I landed that punch on the bag wrong."

"Okay." Skye sighed. "Tell you what," Skye said, stepping back to look at Jordan, "if you agree to have Carly look at your arm."

"No x-rays, though," Jordan pleaded.

"No x-rays," Skye agreed, crossing her fingers behind her back. "I will go to give her a call."

"Okay then," Jordan said, standing up. "I am going to take a shower. Since I cannot train, how about we go for a walk or something?"

"Where were you thinking of walking to?" Skye asked him.

"How about the botanical gardens over in the next town?" Jordan said. "It is not that far away, and I can have Malcolm pack us a picnic lunch. You can see the giant beehive."

"I have wanted to see the giant beehive, but never could find the time" Skye said. "Okay, what time?"

"An hour?" Jordan asked. "That'll give Malcolm enough time to whip something together."

"Great." Skye smiled up at him. "I will go get changed, and that will still give me time to make an appointment for you with Carly."

"Do you think she could come over to the house?" Jordan asked her.

"I am sure she can." Skye gave him a smile before heading to her bedroom.

Deciding to Face Time instead of calling, Skye saw Carly's jaw drop when she told her friend where she was.

"I am surprised that you agreed to take him on as a client after how he dumped your father," Carly told Skye.

"You know how the gym has been struggling, Carly," Skye reassured her friend. "Jordan has paid me on time every week, and these past weeks I have been here have already started to make a difference to the gym's bottom line. So far it's been a win-win."

"As long as it is about the money and building your reputation," Carly breathed. "I don't want to see you getting hurt again by another big-headed jock."

"Says the woman who only seems to date playboy celebrities," Skye joked.

"Honey, you know my philosophy on dating," Carly drawled. "You, though, my dear darling big-hearted friend, tend to wear your emotions on your sleeve."

"Well, my sleeves have been emotionless for a good few years now," Skye assured Carly. "And at this point in my life, I don't have time for relationships. I have a gym to save and a boxer to get ready for his first fight in a week."

"Fine," Carly sighed. "But I am doing this for you to assure that your talent as a trainer shines."

"Understood." Skye saluted her friend. "When can you get here?"

"Well, what time will you be back from your picnic date?" Carly's eyes narrowed in on Skye.

"It's not a date," Skye said, her cheeks flushing. Was it a date? She suddenly wondered. "Since we are not going to train today so he rest his shoulder, we both have some time to kill. So we are going to see the giant beehive and have lunch in the gardens."

"Argh." Carly made a face. "That stupid beehive you have been on about since it opened and never had time."

"Yes, finally," Skye said, grinning at her friend. "At least now you don't have to find excuses to not go see it with me."

"I guess that is an upside to your picnic date," Carly teased Skye with a wink. "Okay, how about seven-thirty tonight?" Carly leaned over her computer, pulled up her appointment schedule, and typed it in. "Too late, you are scheduled."

"I am sure that will be fine," Skye said, shaking her head. "And Carly, this does not mean you can load your fees."

"Never crossed my mind," Carly grinned at Skye. "Well, we don't all have the day off to go frolic with the bees. I have an appointment. Love you, and I will see you tonight. Text me the address." Carly kissed her fingers and touched them to the screen before signing off.

Skye sat staring at the blank screen of her phone, deep in thought. Was this a date? Surely not! Skye chewed her bottom lip. Her heart was beating erratically, and her belly felt all fluttery at the thought of it being a date.

Stop it, Skye! She took a deep breath, trying to calm her wayward emotions. There could never and would never be anything between her and Jordan.

Skye walked over to her closet. Carly had caught her as she was finding something to wear for her outing with Jordan. She did not have much time left. Skye chose a comfortable pair of jeans and a nice shirt. She pulled on her ankle boots and went to dry her hair.

"That beehive was amazing!" Skye's eyes sparkled with excitement. "I have wanted to see it since it opened. But I could never find the time or get someone to go with me, so thank you, Jordan."

"My pleasure," said Jordan, who couldn't help but smiled down at her. Her girlish enthusiasm and utter fascination with the hive was catchy. "I must say you made it a lot more interesting this time around."

"You've seen it before?" Skye looked up at Jordan questioningly.

"Yes. Actually, I was invited to the grand opening," Jordan told her.

Of course he was! That's all it took to jolt Skye back to the real world. Jordan was not only a top sportsman but a celebrity and successful businessman. His world consisted of invitations to important events, spots on TV shows, and ribbon cuttings.

"I think this spot here by the water is a good spot for our picnic," Jordan said, cutting her thoughts and looking at her for confirmation.

"It is beautiful." Skye helped Jordan spread the blanket on the grass.

Skye sat on the soft blanket and looked out over the man-made lake. It sparkled and shimmered lazily in the sun while the ducks, geese, and other types of water birds drifted on its surface.

"Sparkling water?" Jordan poured the beverage into a champagne flute. "At least everyone around will think we are drinking champagne." He laughed and clinked his glass to hers.

"Where does Malcolm manage to find these fresh berries?" Skye enjoyed a few of them. "I struggled to find them at this time of year."

"He has his secret little food sources," Jordan revealed, sharing Malcolm's secret. "But that is all he will say about them, and he is very protective over where they are."

"Ah." Skye smiled, enjoying this relaxed, playful side of Jordan. "I think we should follow him one day and find out. All I end up with are the frozen ones, and although they are nice, there is nothing like fresh fruit or berries."

"I couldn't agree more," Jordan said as he took a handful of berries as well. "So, what does Skye Larsen do for fun?"

"Fun?" Skye raised her eyebrows. "That is something I have not thought about in years now."

"And why not?" Jordan looked at her, amazed. "You know what they say about all work and no fun?"

"That you will be able to keep your business afloat, pay your rent, and put food on the table?" she said innocently.

"Everyone needs downtime, Skye," Jordan said, his facial expression turning serious. "You don't want to look back on your life and have a list full of things you had always wanted to do instead of a list of things you have done."

"Wow." Skye looked at Jordan over the rim of her glass. "That was deep. Even for you."

"I can be deep," Jordan responded, saluting with his glass. "I have many facets to my personality, believe it or not."

"I can see that," Skye teased him, enjoying their afternoon together. "What do you do for fun?"

"Oh, you know, take beautiful women for picnics beside a lake." Jordan grinned cheekily at her. "I also like to go fishing. There is nothing better than going down to the river. Setting out your deck chair, having a nice cold beer, and throwing a baited hook into the water."

"Oh." Skye looked at him, surprised.

"What?" Jordan frowned at her. "Are you going to tell me you are against fishing?"

"No." Skye laughed. "Not at all. My father, Bennie, Amelia, and I used to go fishing in the river all the time." She smiled, thinking about those days. "Nearly every Sunday, in fact. Those were nice days."

"It's good to keep those memories alive," Jordan said, leaning back on his hand with his long legs stretched out in front of him. "It's those types of memories that have kept me going these past five years.

"They can also be the ones that hurt the most," Skye said and smiled sadly. "Because they remind you that those are the things you will never get to do with that person again."

"Not necessarily." Jordan smiled back at her. "If you carry on doing the things you used to do with them, they are still there with you in your heart. It's when you stop doing those things that they hurt."

"Wow." Skye grinned at Jordan. "You are full of good advice and deep, meaningful statements today."

"That punch must have shaken something loose inside my head," Jordan laughed. "Or it could just be that you are so easy to talk to that you bring out my softer side."

"Uh..." Skye pointed at some ducks that seemed to be zoning in on them. "You don't think they want to come and join our picnic, do you?" Her eyes grew more prominent as the birds drew nearer.

"Are you afraid of ducks?'" Jordan looked at her in amazement.

"No," Skye said nervously. "I just don't like their feathers; they give me the creeps."

"What? The ducks or the feathers?" Jordan hid his amusement. She looked so cute, trying to be all brave even though he could see the panic in her eyes. "It is time to pack up and go anyway." Jordan jumped up and started to pack away with Skye's help.

"I still think you need an MRI," Carly informed Jordan. "Your shoulder has some swelling that I am not happy with."

"If it does not go down or is worse after my fight next week, then I will have an MRI," Jordan said as he pulled his shirt back on. "Is there anything I can do for now?"

"Ice, light training, and rest," Carly instructed him, eying his shoulder before turning to Skye. "Can I see his light training schedule for the week leading up to the fight?"

"Sure." Skye walked into the small office Jordan had set aside for her to work in off the gym and a returned with the training schedule in hand. "Here you go."

"Can I keep this?" Carly asked as she scanned through the schedule.

"Yes, it is a copy I made for you," Skye told her.

"Great," Carly said, and began packing up her things. "I will make some changes to this routine and email it you."

"Thank you," Skye said as she helped Carly.

"Only you would hole yourself up with two beautiful women," Quinton called from the gym door. "Hi, I'm Quinton, Jordan's manager, and you are Dr. Carly O'Brien, I take it. It is an honor to meet you."

"Hi." Carly gave Quinton a cool smile. "I have heard of you too from your MMA fighting days and your bad knee injury." Carly automatically glanced down at his knee. "How is it after that groundbreaking treatment you received?"

"Why don't I take you out for dinner, and we can discuss it?" Quinton gave Carly a charming smile.

"I would love to," Carly said with a small smile, "but my schedule is pretty full for the next couple of days."

"Another time then." Quinton was not a little disappointed at being turned down.

"Here." Carly gave him her card, and said, "This is my card. Maybe we can meet up sometime."

"Jordan, I will see you at your fight," Carly said to him. "Skye, I will see you tomorrow night. My mother asked if you could bring your recipe for those protein bars you want her to bake for the store and deli."

"Of course," Skye said as she walked Carly to the car. "Thank you for doing this."

"Anything for you, bestie," Carly said and hugged Skye. "I will see you tomorrow night and email the changes to this schedule first thing tomorrow. Although I think he needs the MRI sooner rather than later, I don't think he should be fighting like that. But hopefully, the light training will bring the swelling down. It could just be a strain."

"Are you trying to convince yourself or me of that?" Skye raised her eyebrows.

"Me, mostly," Carly said, starting up her car. "Love you and see you tomorrow. Don't be late."

"Of course." Skye blew Carly a kiss. "Love you too, Carly."

"I think I love her too," Quinton said from behind, making Skye jump.

"How long have you been standing there eavesdropping?" Skye glared at Quinton.

"Long enough to know the good doctor is worried about our boy's shoulder," Quinton replied, looking down at Skye thoughtfully. "Do you think Jordan should get the MRI?"

"I am not the doctor." Skye shook her head. "And even if we wanted him to, he is not going to get it done before the fight."

"He is rather stubborn," Quinton said, shaking his head.

"I never knew you had a serious knee injury," Skye told him. "Is that why you stopped fighting? You never gave a reason for walking away."

"My knee injury was only part of the reason," he admitted, something clouding his eyes before his charming smile slipped back into place. "I forgot you and the expert doctor there were good friends. Do you think I stand a chance?" he asked, grinning.

"Honestly," Skye began, shaking her head, "I think you two are too much alike to ever be able to connect."

"A female version of me?" Quinton raised his one eyebrow. "How intriguing."

"You are incorrigible." Skye laughed at him.

"Skye," Jordan called from the door. "Dinner is on the table, and Malcolm wants to go home sometime tonight." Jordan came across as a little angry.

"I think that shoulder is making him cranky," Skye said and rolled her eyes. "Goodnight, Quinton."

"Goodnight, Skye." Quinton smiled, watching her walk away. "I don't think it is the shoulder injury that has him cranky," he whistled, laughing to himself.

"You're not going to like this, but I do think you should have an MRI on your shoulder," Skye advised Jordan as they sat at the table, eating dinner. "It is not going to stop you from fighting, but at least we will know if there is any serious damage."

"I appreciate your concern." Jordan smiled at Skye. "I promise to have it checked after my first fight."

"I will hold you to that," Skye said, finishing off her meal. "Well, that is me for the night."

"Me too," Jordan said, sitting back in his chair. "Although it is half of what I usually eat, I am full."

"That is because you are now eating the right foods, and your body has started to function properly again," Skye explained. "I am off to bed. Once again, thank you for taking me to see the giant beehive and the wonderful picnic."

"It was a pleasure and a most enjoyable day," Jordan said, standing up at the same time as Skye. "I know you want to go watch Joey's fight," he told her. "I was going to go to that fight anyway, and Quinton gave me two VIP tickets, as his date canceled on him."

"And Quinton couldn't find another date?" Skye asked in surprise. "Yes, I am going to watch Joey's fight. I am usually one of his team, but Carter will be taking my place for this fight."

"That is good because I would like to go see Joey fight and was wondering if you would like to come with me?" Jordan had no idea why he had prattled to get to the point like a nervous teenager.

"Wow. VIP seats?" Skye asked. "That would be nice, thank you. Since I was not on Joey's team for this match, I was going to ask Carly for her tickets to the fight. Joey wanted you to be there as well."

"Well, now you don't have to ask Carly for her tickets," Jordan said with a smile, walking Skye down the hallway to her room.

"Thank you, Jordan," Skye said. "Goodnight." She walked into her room and closed her door, then leaned against it for a few moments.

Idiot! Her heart was pounding. She could not believe that Jordan had asked her to go out with him twice in one day. She had enjoyed the picnic and seeing that side of him. He seemed normal and down to earth, not some high and mighty athlete out of her reach.

As long as going to the fight together was not a date, was the right thing to do. And although it was not a date-date, Skye was looking forward to Saturday night.

CHAPTER 8
The Mentor

"THIS IS the equipment that I want you to train with for the next week," Carly showed Skye and Jordan around the medical center's super state-of-the-art gym. "I have modified the routine to fit in with this equipment. Skye knows how everything here works, so you are in good hands." Carly called one of her young interns.

"Wow!" Jordan exclaimed, looking around the gym. "Here, I thought that my gym was state-of-the-art."

"As a clinic that specializes in sports injuries and specific training, we have to keep up with the times," Carly clarified, smiling at Jordan. "This is Liam." She pointed to the young intern.

"Liam?" Jordan smiled at the young man. "I didn't realize this was the sports clinic you worked at?"

"Hi, Jordan," Liam said, almost shyly. "Yes, Dr. O'Brien gave me an internship after a boxing injury I sustained last year."

"Oh, that is awesome." Skye smiled at the young man. "What league are you fighting in?"

"I am slowly working my way up," Liam said proudly. "I have seven more fights to go to get to my first championship fight."

"That is awesome, Liam," Jordan told him. "I am glad you took my advice and that Quinton could help you get into those fights."

"Quinton helped him?" Skye looked at Jordan curiously.

"Yes," Jordan explained to Skye how one of the cameramen had introduced Liam to him, and he had been mentoring Liam ever since.

"That is very noble of you," said Skye, smiling at him. "You do have a surprising side to you."

"I am going to take that as a compliment," Jordan said, pretending to catch her words and putting them in his top pocket.

"I will take you through all the equipment and how each of the works," Liam informed them.

"Thank you, Liam," said Skye. "Shall we get started?"

"This is an impressive gym you are working at, Liam," Jordan said as he went through the routine on the last machine. "Are you going to be working with us for the whole week?"

"Yes," Liam told Jordan. "If that is okay with you?"

"Of course." Jordan smiled at him. "I prefer to have someone I know working with me."

"Cool," Liam said as he wrote on Jordan's chart. "I see you are booked in for the fight next week against Granger."

"I believe so." Jordan nodded. "Do you know him?"

"Yes," replied Liam. "I fought him a couple of months ago."

"Oh," Jordan said, finishing his cool down. "How did you do?"

"I beat him," Liam shrugged. "He is tough, fast, and can be a little sneaky."

"Good to know," Jordan said and thanked Liam. "Hey, I will have to speak to Skye first, but you should come and get some training sessions in with us after my first fight."

"I would love that." Liam's eyes lit up. "Thank you."

"Do you have a coach yet?" Jordan asked Liam as he walked to the changing rooms.

"Nah," Liam shrugged. "I am still using whichever coach is available to train me here and out at the other gym where I box."

"You should check out Vic's Gym." Jordan gave Liam the address. "Ask for Bennie and tell him I sent you. The gym belongs to Skye."

"I've heard about Vic's Gym," Liam said as he put the address in his back pocket. "I did not think it was still open as there were rumors of it closing down after the owner died."

"That is Skye's gym," Jordan said, trying to keep his anger in check. It was not the kid's fault he heard the nasty rumors. "It is still very much open."

"I will check it out," Liam said. "Thank you, Jordan. I will see you tomorrow, and I need to go call Dr. O'Brien to let her know you are finished."

"Thanks." Jordan opened his designated locker and pulled off his shirt.

Jordan padded through the locker room with a towel hooked around his waist, his body glistening with droplets of water that had dripped off his damp hair.

"Jordan?" Skye called for him from the door. "Are you in there?"

"Yeah," Jordan called back, clearing his throat as his

stomach muscles clenched and his heart gave a jolt. Having been in a hot shower was not helping him keep his body under control.

"Oh." Skye stopped and swallowed as she stared wide-eyed up at him. "Sorry, I didn't mean to catch you right out of the shower. Liam said you had come in here twenty minutes ago."

"Oh?" Jordan smiled sexily down at her. "So only women can take twenty-minute showers?"

"That's wasting water," Carly said, sauntering into the locker room, holding a thick bandage in her hand. "This is a cold compress bandage. I would like you to wear for the next few days when you are not training."

"That was what I was coming to tell you," Skye announced, her cheeks flushed as her eyes met and held Jordan's.

"Jordan," Carly said, pointing towards a bench. "I need you to sit down here. Skye is going to be putting the bandage on so I can teach her how."

"Fine by me." Jordan breathed, smiling down at Skye until she broke their eye contact to move towards Carly.

Jordan swallowed and breathed quietly for a few minutes. What the hell was wrong with him?

Women had looked at his naked body before. They had even looked at his body with pure lust in their eyes. But never had a woman's eyes felt like they were caressing his body. That is how he felt when he saw her eyes travel up his naked torso.

Jordan gave himself a mental shake. Skye was never going to happen, so he had to get a grip. He felt he was probably reacting this way towards her because she was one of the first females who weren't throwing herself at him. Oh, and Skye's best friend, Dr. Blondie, was another woman who he doubted would throw herself at him, yet she did not affect him this way. Maybe that was because of the cold warning glares Dr. Blondie kept darting at him whenever Skye was near him.

Those looks were enough to douse anyone's passion. The thought made him shudder as he walked over to where the bench was and sat down.

"Can you lift your arm like this," Carly said, positioning his arm. "You are going to have to hold it like that for a while."

"Sure," Jordan said distractedly.

Jordan's breath caught in his throat as Skye's warm, soft hand touched his collarbone. His Adam's apple bobbed in his throat as he swallowed, trying hard to get his mind on something else and not Skye's hand on his bare skin. If he had thought her eyes caressing him played havoc with his body, her actual touch was torture. All he could think of was grabbing her and crushing his lips against her soft, red ones while pulling her close to him.

STOP IT! His mind screamed at him. Think about boxing —nope, that brought up images of Skye in her tight training gear. He shook his head.

"Are you okay?" Skye's voice drifted through his ear.

"Yes," he said, clearing his throat as his voice came out like a squeak. "My arm is throbbing a bit." That was not a lie; if truth be told, it ached like hell, but even that pain could not take his mind of Skye's hands on his body as she wrapped the bandage around his chest and arm.

"Well then, it's lucky that Skye is finished now," Carly chipped in, stepping back and looking at him with knowing eyes. "Does it feel comfortable?"

"It's fine." Jordan moved his shoulders and body to get a feel for the bandage.

"Good. We wouldn't want it cutting off any of your blood flow now, would we?" Carly's eyes bore into Jordan."

"It's all good," said Jordan, who was smiling at Carly. "Now, would you ladies excuse me? I have to get dressed, or Skye and I will be late for our date." He gave Carly a smug smile over Skye's head.

"Of course." Carly glared right back at him. "Skye and I have some options for you to discuss." She smiled back at him before walking Skye out of the locker room.

That woman did not like Jordan one little bit. He knew it. As soon as they were out of the door, Jordan sighed in relief. Good grief. How was he going to endure having his bandage changed by Skye every day for the next five days without losing his mind or scaring her off?

"Carly gets into these fights, doesn't she?" Jordan laughed as he watched Carly scream for Joey on the outside of the cage.

"Oh, yes." Skye nodded. "Especially when it has to do with Joey. She is very invested in him; the clinic is one of his sponsors."

"Joey is good. He moves like lightning, and he has excellent instincts." Jordan watched the younger man block a blow and then turn the counter by flooring his opponent. "Go, Joey," Jordan shouted. He could not help himself between how good the kid was and Skye's enthusiasm. He had gotten right on board with the fight.

In the final round, Joey took down his opponent and won the fight. When the fighter exited the ring, Joey grabbed the door frame and lifted his leg. Skye and Jordan watched helplessly while Carter and Carly rushed to his side.

"We have to go," Skye announced as she stood up and ran towards where Joey's team members were carrying him.

"What happened?" Skye called to Carly, craning her neck around the giant man blocking her from getting to Joey.

"I'm not sure," Carly said, coming to where Skye and Jordan were standing. "But I think it's his tendon again."

"I knew he was not ready for the fight," Skye hissed. "Damn these stubborn men."

"I am going to take him to the clinic. Bennie is calling his mother, who is going to meet us there." Carly turned to hold up her hand to the person calling. "I have to go. I will call you later."

"Please do," Skye called after Carly. "I knew he should not fight tonight. I could see when he spared or even walked that he was favoring that leg."

"Hey, you did all you could," Jordan said, gently rubbing her arms comfortingly from where he stood towering behind her. "I think we should do what Carly said and go home and wait for her call."

"You're right," Skye turned and looked up at Jordan. "This is what happens when I do not run things."

"No," Jordan told her sternly. "This was not Joey's trainer's or your fault. He felt like he could fight, and he did. He even won, so he knew how hard he could push his body."

"Staring at the phone is not going to make Carly call," Jordan said softly. "I am sure Joey is going to be okay."

"I know." Skye put her phone down on the coffee table.

"Why don't we take your mind off Joey for a while?" Jordan's voice was deep and seductive. "Tell me about Skye."

"Only if you return the favor and tell me a bit more about you." Skye smiled at his grin.

"Deal," Jordan agreed. "But I get to ask the first question."

"Okay," Skye said, narrowing her eyes at him, wondering what he was going to ask her.

"You never speak about your mother." Jordan gave her a gentle smile. "What happened to her?"

"My mother and father got married when they were still quite young," Skye explained. "My mother fell pregnant with me when she was nineteen, so my mom and dad, who had been high school sweethearts, got married."

"That was a big sign of the times back then," Jordan said, before picking up his bottle of water.

"They were together until I was five," Skye took a sip of her water. "My mother was not what you would call 'motherly.' Although she did try." She looked down, fidgeting with the mouth of her water bottle. "She never wanted kids; she was always too ambitious and wanted to go on archeological digs."

"She was an archeologist?" Jordan looked impressed.

"Yes, she would rather be digging in the dirt than be with her own daughter." Skye smiled sadly. "But that was okay as I had my dad, Bennie, and eventually Amelia."

"Amelia was Bennie's wife?" Jordan frowned as he tried to remember her.

"Yes." Skye smiled fondly. "She was also the only mother figure I had in my life growing up."

"So your mother just got up and left you?" Anger burned through Jordan's gut.

Jordan could not understand how a mother could ever leave her child. You had to be rather cold to do it. Although there were circumstances where it could not be helped, this did not seem to be one of those circumstances.

"She would send me things from her digs," Skye said, remembering the postcards and a few letters. "But soon, they stopped. I did look her up once." The pain dulled Skye's beautiful eyes for a few seconds. "She had moved on and had a new family."

"A new family?" Jordan's brows creased.

"Yes, for someone who did not like kids, she had four." Skye could not help the little bit of anger that split into her voice when she thought of that. "I never saw or heard from her again."

"I know she is your mom, Skye," Jordan soothed. He

could not believe a mother could be so callous, "but it sounds to me like you were better off without her."

"That is what Amelia said," Skye said smiling. "She came with me to find my mother. She was not very nice to my mother either when I was coldly told I should have called first."

"No way," Jordan hissed; he had never deliberately hit a woman before, but he would like to slap some sense and maternal instinct into Skye's mother.

"It was fine." Skye smiled sadly. "At first, I did not understand how a mother could turn her back on their child without any remorse whatsoever."

"Your dad, Bennie, and his wife did an excellent job of raising you," Jordan complimented her. "And you got to have three parents, not just two or one."

"I was one of the lucky ones." Skye smiled, nodding. "I know that. I watched my friends throughout school and college being devastated by their parents' sudden divorce."

"There is nothing sudden about getting a divorce," Jordan said, shaking his head. "That is something that brews like a slow-boiling pot left on the stove."

"I couldn't agree more with you there." Skye sniffed, fighting off the tears. How stupid was she to still want to cry over a divorce that happened almost two decades ago?

"I am sorry about your mother, Skye," Jordan said softly. "I know what it is like to lose a parent."

"Did you lose your parents?" Skye asked Jordan. "I thought your mother and father were still alive. Aren't they coming for dinner tomorrow night?"

"Yes, but those are my adoptive parents," Jordan explained to Skye. "My real parents died when I was seven."

"Oh no, Jordan, what happened?" Skye wanted to reach out and comfort Jordan so badly that she had to dig her nails into her palms to stop herself from doing so.

Jordan stared into her eyes, which were burning with compassion for him. Not with pity, like so many others who looked at him when they learned about his childhood. Skye was filled with compassion and a deeper understanding of his pain as they had shared almost the same pain. Loss of a parent or parents at a young and tender age—a time of your life when your physical, emotional, and mental development depended on parental love. A love that was much like the sun and water were to a budding flower.

"My parents were both in the army," Jordan told Skye. "My mother was killed on assignment, and four months later, my father died of a heart attack during a training exercise."

"Oh no." Skye did not have the words to express her sorrow for seven-year-old Jordan. "What a terrible twist of fate." She reached out and cupped his hands in hers in a gesture of comfort.

"I usually stayed with my father's best friend when my parents were away on assignment," Jordan continued, smiling, enjoying the feel of her warm hands around his hands. "Because I had no one else to go to, the Perkins family adopted me."

"That was kind of them," said Skye, her eyes sparkling with unshed tears. "What a tragic story, Jordan."

"I learned to box around that age." Jordan absently played with Skye's fingers. "It was a way to let out my anger and pain. I was good at it."

"You were very passionate about your boxing." Skye could remember watching him train when her father was his coach. "Why did you stop?"

"My brother, the Perkins's son, Wayne, was killed that year," Jordan revealed, his eyes shadowed with grief. "

"I'm sorry, Jordan." Skye looked shocked. "I did not know. I thought you just walked away."

"I did," said Jordan, nodding. "Wayne followed me to

every fight no matter where that fight was. He believed that it was important for someone from the family to be there if something happened."

"It seems like you hit the jackpot when it came to brothers," Skye told Jordan, giving him a warm smile.

"I did. That goes for my sister as well." Jordan smiled. "Paige is the best."

"Malcolm agrees with you on that one," Skye teased him, trying to lighten the mood. "Or he is scared of her champion fighter brother."

"Wayne used to box as well," Jordan told Skye. "We would spar all the time. In fact, he would come to my training sessions if he could get off work early."

"Yes." It suddenly dawned on Skye. "I remember him."

"At my last fight, Wayne could not get a flight to it, so he drove all the way to the tournament." Jordan swallowed and linked his fingers with Skye's as his mind went back to that fateful night. "He was exhausted, but he had to be back at a certain time for a meeting the following day.

"Oh, no, Jordan," Skye said, realizing where this was going. She had heard about people being overtired and falling asleep at the wheel.

"I told him I would get him a plane ticket or bus ticket and drive his car back for him," Jordan said, running his free hand through his hair. "But Wayne was as stubborn as could be and insisted he was fine. He had only been driving for an hour when he fell asleep at the wheel. His car cut across the highway and was hit by an oncoming truck."

The room fell silent as Jordan and Skye sat with their hands linked, each lost in thought. The silence was broken by the ringing of Skye's phone. Jordan felt somehow cheated when she gently pulled her hand away to answer.

"It's Carly," Skye covered the mouthpiece to say.

"I will go get some more water," Jordan told Skye with a

tight smile. He was feeling a little strange, almost angry that Carly had disturbed their moment. He got up and left Skye to speak to Carly.

"Well, at least it is just a strain and nothing more serious," Skye told Jordan as he walked her to her room. "Thank you, Jordan. I have had a wonderful evening."

"I did too. You are a very easy person to talk to," Jordan said softly, his eyes capturing hers.

They both stood up and faced each other, getting lost in each other's eyes for a few seconds before Skye reached up and kissed him on the cheek.

"Goodnight, Jordan," she said, smiling at him before disappearing into her bedroom.

Jordan stood rooted to the spot, staring at her door, his heart pounding in his chest. When had he ever hesitated to kiss a woman before? His subconscious screamed back, *When that woman means more to you than a one-night stand!*

He gave himself another mental shake before padding off to his room. It was going to be yet another sleepless night filled with thoughts of Skye.

CHAPTER 9
Flowers for Skye

LIAM HAD BEEN TRAINING with Jordan for the whole week; the next day was a rest day with some light warm-ups and stretches, and the following day was Jordan's first fight. Skye was a boiling pot of emotions about Jordan and the fight. She had been rather jumpy around him. The night of Joey's fight, they had seemed to get closer, but they were a little awkward around each other the next day.

Skye had decided to just act normal and keep their relationship on the level it had been these past weeks she had been training him. They soon fell back into their usual rhythm.

If Skye was being honest, she would admit that she had spent many nights tossing and turning, thinking about Jordan. Her dreams were even plagued by him. Every time he walked into a room, her heart would do cartwheels, and she would feel like the world had become a little brighter.

Put a lid on this, Skye! She gave herself a stern talk too. You know nothing could ever happen. He has all the lifestyle of the rich and famous, with a calendar filled with social commitments, work meetings, this charity event, and now a new boxing career. Skye sighed. That was not her idea of the recipe for a happily ever after scenario or even a good relationship.

That evening, she had been roped into going to a function to promote his upcoming fight. Jordan had invited all those closest to her, including Joey, Carly, and Liam, as his guests. It was a black-tie event, and Skye had no idea what she was going to wear. Skye had tossed her wardrobe when Declan had dumped her a few years ago. She had sworn then to never go to one of these types of events again, but it looked like she was about to break her vow.

Carly was going to take her shopping after Jordan's training session to get Skye something to wear. That in itself was daunting to Skye. She hated clothes shopping, and her idea of accessorizing was changing her Fitbit. Skye had managed to talk Carly out of making her go to a hair salon. Skye was happy with Miss Farley's hair salon down the road from her gym, and she was going to go there for a quick styling a little later in the day.

"Okay," Liam said, jolting Skye out of her reverie. "Here you go; just need your signature. Jordan has gone into the shower, so he should be ready in about thirty minutes or so. That dude takes forever in a shower." Liam shook his head as he made his way to go find Carly.

"Oh, come on, Skye." Carly pushed her into the dressing room and handed her three dresses. "Just try them on for me."

"None of these dresses is my style." Skye held the first dress up. "How does this one even stay where it's supposed to stay? I can already see it falling down."

"Skye, that is the beauty of having a petite body like

yours," Carly said, pushing Skye into the cubical and closing the door. "Try that one on first."

"You would say that," Skye said as she pulled off her gym gear and put on the black dress.

Skye looked at herself in the mirror and could not believe how well the dress fit her. It flowed over her small body, giving her a soft, sexy, feminine shape. The front dipped in a cowl that hung low between her breasts while the body clung to her, ending mid-thigh to show off her shapely, toned legs. The shoestring straps highlighted her delicate collarbones and long, swan-like neck, while the rear of the dress dipped down to her lower back.

Skye turned around in the dress. It was gorgeous.

"What are you doing in there?" Carly called to her. "I want to see!"

Skye opened the door and walked out. Carly gasped.

"Oh my word, Skye." Carly was amazed. "This is the dress."

"I still have a few others to try on," Skye said, pointing to the other dresses Carly had shoved her into the changing room with. "What if I like one of them more than this one?"

"Seriously?" Carly folded her arms and looked at Skye with raised eyebrows. "Do you think any of those are going to top this one?"

"Maybe" Skye was feeling a little self-conscious.

"Sorry, but that's the one." Carly pushed Skye back into the cubicle. "Let's go pay for it before you change your mind, and then we'll go find you some accessories."

"Carly, have you seen the price tag on this dress?" Skye came out of the cubicle with the dress over her arm. "There is no way I can afford this," she whispered.

"Well, I can." Carly took it from Skye. "And before you have one of your little girl stubborn bouts, you are my friend, and this is my treat to you."

"I can't accept that, Carly," Skye cried out, stomping after her friend.

"You can and you will," Carly said, looking at her friend. "Besides, I figure you owe me for taking on Jordan. So this is how you are going to repay me."

"That makes absolutely no sense whatsoever," Skye retorted, glaring at Carly.

"It does to me," she replied.

"Please, Carly, that is more than I make in two months."

"Really?" Carly gave the cashier her credit card. "Then you need to up your rates because I am more than sure Jordan can afford to pay you more than that."

"Carly!" Skye sighed. "Thank you." She gave her friend a peck on the cheek.

"Like I've told you time and time again, that is what I am here for," Carly reminded her friend, who was trying to balance the entire world on her shoulders.

"I know," Skye said, smiling at the woman who was her lifelong best friend. "You have always been my rock."

"And you mine." Carly linked her arm through Skye's as they continued down the street for an afternoon of shopping.

Skye looked at herself in the mirror. She could not believe that she was the same person in the mirror. She grinned, thinking about the salon battle she and Carly had earlier. They eventually ended up going to Miss Farley's hair salon. Skye had enjoyed the look on Carly's face when Brenda, Miss Farley's niece, had done her hair. She was fresh out of beauty school and amazing. She had big plans for the hair salon that her aunt wanted her to take over in the future.

Carly's and Skye's hair, skin, and nails looked fabulous, and the best part was that Brenda was about to get an influx of high-profile clients, thanks to Carly. Skye smiled as she secured the thin gold and diamond bracelet Amelia had left to her. Tears welled up in her eyes as she remembered the day she told Amelia how much she liked her bracelet. "Well, sweetheart," Amelia had said, "one day it will be yours!"

She sniffed and got a tissue to dab her eyes carefully so as not to ruin her makeup that had been artfully applied by Brenda.

Skye sat on the bed, looking at the shoes Carly had coerced her to get. They matched her dress perfectly, but Skye was not sure she would be able to walk in such high heels. She was used to sneakers, which enabled her to have her entire foot on the ground, not just parts of it.

The doorbell rang, and Skye looked at her wristwatch, another heirloom from Amelia— one she only wore on special occasions. It was a delicate gold watch that had been left to Amelia by her grandmother. She swallowed the lump in her throat; it was times like these that she felt the loss of her father and Amelia the most.

"Skye," Jordan called to her as he knocked on her door. "The limo is here with the rest of our party in it."

"I will be right there shortly." Skye stood, trying not to wobble too much in the ridiculously high heels, grabbed her coat, and pulled open her door.

Her throat went dry as the tantalizing scent of Jordan's cologne teased her senses. She swallowed as her eyes traveled up over his tuxedo-clad body. Oh, my word! Skye's heart seemed to stop beating at the sight of Jordan's finely toned body in an immaculately tailored suit.

"Wow!" said Jordan, who was floored by the sight of Skye in the most provocative and tantalizing dress he was sure he had ever seen. Well, he had seen similar dresses on many women, but none of them wore it quite as well as Skye did. She was gorgeous! He cleared his throat. "You look amazing," he breathed, congratulating himself for not squeaking.

"Thank you," Skye said softly. "You don't look half bad yourself in your tuxedo."

"Thank you," Jordan said and gave a small bow, glad that she had broken the tension. "Shall we?" He offered her his arm but immediately regretted it as her hand curled around his biceps. He felt his pulse go crazy. This was going to be a long night!

"I feel like I am off to the prom," Skye said, her gaze drawn to the stretch limo.

They seemed to be on the same wavelength. Right now, Jordan felt like a teenager on his first date, complete with raging hormones.

"After you," he said as he held the door open for her, taking a sharp breath once he spotted the back of Skye's dress that showed off the soft curve and the pale skin of her back. He squeezed his eyes shut, clenching his jaw as he breathed, fighting to regain control of his wayward body.

"Oh, wow!" Skye was sure everyone in the limo shouted at once, making her feel very self-conscious.

"Champagne?" Carly offered Skye, knowing how much her friend hated being in the spotlight.

"Please." Skye grabbed the flute and swallowed, holding up the glass for a refill.

"Are you sure?" Carly asked, eyeing her friend. "You know how this stuff gives you migraines."

"Thanks, Dr. O'Brien," Skye mocked. "But I think I know my limit."

"Okay then." Carly poured Skye another glass of champagne.

Skye stood back, sipping on a glass of sparkling water as she watched Quinton and Jordan do the rounds. Her head was already throbbing from all the flash photography of the sports magazines that had been assigned the exclusive for the event. She did not know how he handled all this—the press, being mobbed by fans, and having to attend these kinds of events regularly. Jordan's whole life was like one big photo shoot.

"I thought that was you," a deep, familiar voice from her past had her balling her fist at her side and clenching her jaw. "You look amazing."

"Hello, Declan," Skye turned to greet her ex-fiancé, pro-footballer Declan Bell. "You are looking well yourself."

"Ouch." Declan put a hand over his heart. "There was a time you would tell me how handsome I looked all cleaned up." He gave her a boyish grin.

"I didn't think you would come to a boxing event," Skye said, ignoring Declan's hint for a compliment. "I thought you hated the archaic sport of punching someone in the face?"

"I did not say that exactly," Declan defended himself. "We are here because the company promoting this event is looking to buy out our team."

"What?" Skye looked at Declan questioningly. "The company sponsoring this event is Wayward Sporting Apparel."

"Yup." Declan smiled. "Seems like Jordan Turner is looking to expand into football now."

"Oh, I did not know that," Skye said, looking over at Jordan, who was signing an autograph for a brunette who was devouring him with her eyes. Red heat burned through Skye's veins as Jordan flirted with the woman. Relax, Skye, what do you care who Jordan flirts with? Not your concern.

"Can you believe that guy?" Declan stared at Jordan. "Coming out of retirement after five years like he was some kind of legend."

"Actually," Skye turned to face Declan, "he was a legend

and walked away from his career undefeated. And you really should not be talking like that about a man who potentially holds your career in his hands."

"Geez," Declan looked at her, taken aback by her outburst. "Relax. The man has got a lot of guts to be doing this. But at his age, the boxers he is going to be up against are younger and faster."

"Since when did you become an expert in boxing?" Skye frowned at him.

"Since I got engaged to an MMA fighter," Declan smiled at him in shock. "Pam Riddle, you may have heard of her."

"You're Pam Riddle's mystery celebrity man." Skye looked at Declan in amazement. "Declan, that is fantastic!" she exclaimed.

Declan may be an arrogant dick, but they had a lot of history, and she was happy for him.

"I meant to call you," Declan said, looking a little bit uneasy. "I know we left things between us in quite a mess."

"It's okay, Declan," Skye told him. "We've both moved on. It is all water under the bridge."

"I'm glad you said that," Declan breathed a sigh of relief. "Because Pam asked if you would be happy to take her on as a client at Vic's Gym."

Skye nearly choked on her sparkling water. She stared at Declan, wondering if her ears were deceiving her. Pam Riddle had changed Declan—not only was he a little less conceited, but he also asked Skye for a favor. Skye gaped at him for a few seconds before it dawned on her.

"Oh." Skye nodded, her eyes narrowing in on. "Now that I have Carter Barnes training Joey and I am training Jordan, all of a sudden Vic's Gym is appealing to you? Even though it's being run by a woman?"

"What?" It was Declan's turn to look shocked. "Back up there a bit, Skye," he looked at her with surprise.

"Oh, come on." Skye shook her head at him. "You don't think I am that naive to think that you suddenly grew enough confidence in my training or my ability to run a gym to accommodate someone on Pam's level, did you?" she looked at him angrily before turning to walk away.

"No, Skye," Declan said, grabbing her arm. "Please, wait a minute. Just hear me out."

"You have five minutes," Skye told Declan, coldly.

"I never said I did not have confidence in your coaching abilities. You are an amazing coach." Declan held onto the top of her arms. "Look how you helped me with my throw? I merely suggested that running a gym would be a little over your head. Especially as we were engaged to be married. I just did not think you would have the time to dedicate to it."

"Oh, really?" Skye could not believe he thought her whole life had to revolve around him. "I feel sorry for Pam then. What are you going to do? Are you going to tell her to give up her career to follow you around and keep your ego inflated?"

"No." Declan took a deep breath and let go of Skye's arms to run a hand through his hair in exasperation. "I am coming off all wrong here, aren't I?"

"I would say so," a female voice purred from behind Skye; she turned to find Pam Riddle standing behind her with a smile on her face.

"Pam Riddle," Skye swallowed. Pam was one of her favorite MMA fighters.

"Hi, Skye," Pam smiled down at her. "I am so glad to meet you. I have heard so much about you."

"I hope you don't believe everything you hear?" Skye said, smiling at the woman. She was even more gorgeous in person. The sporting magazines had dubbed her the princess of MMA.

"Trust me." Pam smiled. "It has only ever been good

things. My father has read all your papers on your training methods and is impressed."

"Professor Riddle has read my papers?" Skye stared at Pam wide-eyed. Pam's father was one of the topmost authorities on sports science.

"Yes, and now that I live in the same town as you, I would like you to take me on as a client." Pam's face changed to one of concern as Skye's face paled. "Are you okay?"

"Yes." Skye looked at Pam, star-struck. "You want me to train you?"

"Yes." Pam nodded. "Not this season, though, as I am out of the ring for a couple of months." She smiled and rubbed her stomach.

"You're pregnant?" Skye breathed stupidity.

"Yes," Pam smiled, meeting Declan's eyes lovingly. "We are getting married next month. Did Declan give you the invites?"

"Invites?" Skye felt like she was in some sort of alternate reality. Things like this did not happen to her.

"Yes," Declan confirmed, pulling out the invites from his pocket. "There is one for Carly, Bennie, that kid, Joey, and you."

"Did I hear you say you were training Jordan Turner?" Pam asked her. "His excellent training coach is you?"

"I don't know about that." Skye laughed, feeling a little self-conscious. "But yes, I have been training him. I thought you knew, and that is why Declan asked me to have you as a client." Skye frowned at Pam. "Or is it because Carter Barnes is helping me out at the gym?"

"Carter Barnes?" Both Pam and Declan exclaimed at once.

"I thought that is what I heard you say," Declan said, amazed. "How do you know Carter Barnes?"

"Bennie used to be his trainer when he first started," Skye explained. "As Carter's career was taking off, Bennie's wife got sick, so he introduced Bennie to a new coach."

“I’m sorry. I did not know that.” Declan looked a little ashamed.

“So,” Pam linked her arm through Skye’s, maneuvering her through the crowd. “What do you say? Can you take me on as a client?”

“Of course,” Skye said, looking up at Pam, amazed, “I would be honored.”

“No, the honor is mine,” Pam assured her, stopping in front of a tall man who was speaking to a group of people. “I have someone I would like you to meet.”

Upon hearing Pam’s voice, the man turned around. For the second time that night, Skye was a bit star-struck. Patrick Riddle smiled down at Skye.

“Dad,” Pam said. “I would like you to meet.”

“Skye Larsen,” he said, with a charming smile. “It is a pleasure to meet you, my dear. I have been following your papers on your training methods, and I think they are brilliant.”

Skye sat on a stool at the bar. It felt as if she was in a dream. She could not believe how the night had turned out. A meeting she had dreaded had turned out a lot better than she ever thought it would. She had met two people, whom if she had made a list of people to meet, they wouldn’t be on it. And she had landed a new high-profile customer for the gym and been invited to write a paper with a man who had inspired her to take sports science.

“What are you grinning about?” Joey plopped onto the barstool next to her.

“I got us a new customer for the gym.” Skye beamed at him.

“Cool.” Joey nodded. “We need some more of those.”

“I think once the word about Jordan spreads, we will get

some more in." Skye turned toward Joey, barely able to contain her excitement. "But when word gets out, we have two high-profile customers..."

"Who is the other high-profile customer?" Joey looked at her suspiciously.

"Someone whose wedding we have all been invited to," Skye announced, pulling out his and Bennie's wedding invitations.

"Do you mean Declan?" Joey gave her a look. "Seriously, you don't want to get involved with that man again. Skye, look at what he did to you the last time."

Oh, no," Skye frowned, shaking her head. "Not Declan, his fiancée."

"Okay, now I'm curious to know who the poor woman is," Joey said as he ripped open the invitation and nearly fainted. "Pam Riddle." He breathed. "Pam Riddle is going to be coached at our gym?"

Skye nodded; she could not stop grinning. She would finally be able to take the gym to the next level and keep her home.

"Skye, this is huge!" Joey jumped off the barstool excitedly. "Carter is going to have a fit."

"You can't go telling anyone just yet," Skye playfully warned him. "And for goodness sake, stop bouncing on your ankle like that. You don't want to have to sit the next fight out."

"Can I meet her?" Joey stopped bouncing to look pleadingly at Skye with his big puppy dog eyes.

"Okay. But no drooling over her, okay?" Skye warned him.

"No, wait." Joey stopped, his face becoming serious. "Isn't it going to be weird for you, with Declan being your ex and all?"

"No." Skye's heart swelled joy. He was willing to forgo meeting one of his idols for her. "That ship sailed years ago,

Joey. But it is really sweet of you to care. Now come on, before she leaves."

Skye brushed her teeth and padded towards her bed. Her feet ached from wearing those torturous shoes the entire night. Although the night had not been a total disaster for her, she was a little disappointed that she had barely seen or spoken to Jordan throughout the whole evening.

When she had left, he had been nowhere in sight. She did not know if she should wait for him or not. But she was tired; her head was starting to ache as badly as her feet were. She had caught a lift home with Carly, who had been ecstatic about Pam signing on as her new client. It was not too much of a surprise to know that Pam was also one of Carly's clinic's customers.

Skye sat on the bedside and put her gold watch and bracelet into their boxes before closing them in the bedside drawer. Her mind was filled with thoughts of Jordan and the way he seemed to shine in the spotlight like that was what he was born for. Her stomach knotted every time she thought of the women who threw themselves at him the entire night. She sighed; she had known she was in trouble when she saw how he had looked at her tonight. She had to pull herself together and remind herself that their relationship was strictly business —no more impromptu outings and nights of intimate conversations.

Skye was just about to switch off her light and get into bed when she heard a soft knock at her door.

"Skye?" Jordan called to her from the other side of the door. "I saw your light on. Are you still awake?"

Skye took a deep, steady breath, pulling on her robe before opening her door.

"Is there something wrong?" Skye asked Jordan as coolly as she could, staying as neutral as possible.

"I..." Jordan frowned down at her. "I wanted to give you these." He pulled a bunch of flowers from behind his back. "Thank you for everything."

"They are lovely, Jordan," Skye said as she took the flowers. "But there is no need to thank me. I am just doing what you pay me to do." She gave him a tight smile. Why did she just say that?

"Right," Jordan replied, something clouding his eyes for a second before he gave her a tight smile. "Well, I will let you get back to bed."

"Goodnight, Jordan." Skye thanked him for the flowers and closed her bedroom door.

CHAPTER 10
The Ghost of Wayne

JORDAN WAS FEELING a little bit tired, not having slept too well the previous night. He still couldn't understand why Skye had become all frosty after he thought they were getting closer.

Could it be that she still had feelings for Declan Bell? Jordan thought, as he had seen them talking together for quite a while at the event the previous night. The thought of Skye with Declan brought knots to his stomach. What the hell was wrong with him?

"Jordan?" Skye was looking at him questioningly. "I asked you if your shoulder was still giving you problems."

"No," Jordan lied, not noticing her coming in. "It has been fine these past two days," he told her with a reassuring smile.

"You look tired," Skye said softly. "I think you need to get some rest today."

"Sure." Jordan gave a small nod.

Did she think he was going to be able to rest? Jordan thought. Not only was his first fight tomorrow, but his mind was plagued with thoughts of her, and it was the anniversary of Wayne's death on the same day as the fight.

"Okay," said Skye, as she eyed him out strangely. "You take it easy in the morning and try to get some sleep. I have to go to the gym to discuss some business with Bennie and Carter, but I will be back before three to have a light workout and sort out the finer details for tomorrow."

"Fine," Jordan said abruptly. "I will see you then." He turned and left the kitchen without another word, leaving Skye staring at him curiously.

"You won, little brother." Wayne grinned at Jordan. "I couldn't be more proud of my little brother," he said as he wrapped his arm around Jordan's neck to rub his head.

"You are so lucky I am so beat from that fight." Jordan laughed, freeing himself from Jordan's grip. "Your encouragement always gets me through the fight." Jordan hugged his older brother. "Thanks, bro."

"You know what I always say." Wayne looked at Jordan. "Family comes first, no matter what. I have not missed a fight yet; there was no way I was going to let grounded flights make me miss your big fight."

"We are heading off to get something to eat once my eye has been patched up." Jordan grimaced when Wayne reached up to judge how deep the cut was.

"Ouch. That was quite a punch you took there, brother," Wayne whistled. "Thank goodness you have such a hard head."

"I had to give the amount of time I landed on it with you making me do all those stunts for your movie scenes." Jordan laughed. "So, I think you should thank me the most when you make your speech at the awards ceremony for best director."

"I don't know if it is mine yet." A flash of excitement flittered into Wayne's eyes. "But here's hoping."

"We all know it's yours," Jordan said encouragingly. His brother had worked hard to achieve the success he had; no one deserved that award as much as he did.

"Go get that cut looked at." Wayne waved Jordan off. "I will meet you in your hotel lobby. I am going to get freshened up. I need to drive back as soon as dinner is over."

"Are you sure you won't stay the night?" Jordan looked at Wayne worriedly. "You have not slept in almost forty-eight hours now."

"You know me," Wayne dismissed Jordan's concerns. "I can go for a week without too much sleep. Now, go get patched up. I will see you at the hotel."

Jordan watched Wayne walk away. He did not feel good about letting his brother drive back to their hometown, not having had any sleep in over two days.

"I've made arrangements to drive back with you tonight," Jordan said with a smile to his brother. "I thought you could use the company, and I cut down on the cost of another flight."

"No." Wayne shook his head at Jordan. "You have that big event tomorrow. You have to be there; it is important for your career."

"It is just a promotional event." Jordan shrugged. "There is nothing in the rule books that say I have to be there to line up my next fight."

"Come on, Jordan," Wayne told him, with a more serious tone. "You have worked your butt off to get here. I am not going to let you jeopardize that because you are worried about my sleeping habits.

"I can't let my brother drive when he is exhausted," Jordan argued. "That would be irresponsible and selfish of me."

"I tell you what," Wayne began to make a deal with Jordan, "I will drive halfway and book into a motel. I will get some sleep and finish the drive home tomorrow in time for my big meeting about that new movie if you agree to stay and attend that event tomorrow?"

"I don't know, Wayne." Jordan eyed his brother out. "Are you going to be okay to even drive halfway?"

"Jordan," Wayne breathed, "little bro, I am fine."

The flash of the cameras went off in his face like firecrackers. The reporters surrounded him like piranhas rounding in on their prey. Security guards formed a tight ring around Jordan as he rushed up the stairs to the hospital.

The glass door slid open, but Jordan hesitated to take the step inside because he knew that when he did, it would make what the voice on the other side of his say all too real.

"Mr. Turner?" A nurse walked up to him. She smiled warmly at him, holding out her hand. "Please, come this way."

He followed the nurse down the cold, sterile halls of the hospital to the ICU unit. His parents and sister were sitting outside the room. Guilt and shame ripped through him when he saw the devastation on their faces. This was his fault, and they all knew it. If only he had insisted on driving Wayne home, his brother would not be lying in that bed with a machine keeping him alive.

Wayne had died on the way to the hospital and had been revived, but he had been down for too long. Wayne was clinically brain dead, and the family was being pushed to take him off life support as he was an organ donor.

Jordan looked through the window into the ICU ward.

His brother had a tube coming out of his mouth, and there were machines making all kinds of noises that Jordan could hear from where he was. Memories of waving Wayne off a few hours ago tormented his mind.

"Go get that belt, little brother, and make me proud!" were the last words Wayne had uttered to Jordan.

"Oh, son." Jordan's mother held her arms open for him, tears streaming down her soft cheeks.

"Mom," Jordan knelt in front of her, gripping her in a crushing hug. "I am so sorry, mom." His mom had stroked his hair and rocked him like she did whenever he would have a bad dream as a little boy.

Jordan's father and sister, Paige, all joined in the hug as they sobbed together, their hearts broken and a piece of their family torn from them. The doctor interrupted them, apologizing for being callous and then guilting them about saving a teenager's life with Wayne's heart.

Watching as the doctors stopped the life support was the worst moment of Jordan's life. The machine that bleeped, teasing them with its ups and downs, only to mock them when it flat-lined, had made Jordan want to jam his fist through it. When they had wheeled Wayne out of the room to take him apart, organ by organ, Jordan had snapped.

WAYNE!

Jordan screamed, as he jolted to a sitting position on the bed. Sweat beaded down his naked torso, his heart going wild in his chest. He got up to go splash water on his face. He padded back into the room, noticing he had not even slept for an hour.

"Jordan?" There was a light knock at the door before it

cracked open, and Skye peeked in. "Are you okay?" She hesitantly made her way into his room. "I heard you shout out."

He stood staring at her, his heart still racing in his chest as the memories of his brother's accident swirled through his mind.

Skye frowned up at him while walking towards him.

"Jordan?" Skye looked worriedly up at him. "Are you..."

He could not help himself; he reached out and grabbed her. Pulling her to him, his lips found hers in a soul-crushing kiss. His heart beat accelerated even more as his body ached with the need for her.

An alarm bell went off in his brain, becoming increasingly louder and louder until the sound registered to him as his phone through the fog of desire. He suddenly pulled back and stared—dumbfounded—at Skye, who was staring at him just as shocked.

The phone trilled once more, but he ignored it.

"Skye..." Jordan was about to apologize, but she stepped forward and reached up to kiss him again. He pulled his head back to look at her, desire emanating from his eyes. He whispered in a hoarse voice, "Are you sure?"

Skye smiled seductively at him and wrapped her arms around his neck to pull his head down while he grabbed her, lifting her so she could wrap her legs around his waist. Their lips met once again in a passionate kiss that made the rest of the world melt away. He spun around and dropped onto the bed on his back, with Skye on top of him.

His phone rang again, interrupting their blissful moment. Skye rolled off Jordan, giving a small laugh.

"You had better answer that," Skye said, her voice laced with passion, just like Jordan's was.

Jordan took a deep breath before picking up his phone to see that it was his mother calling.

Skye indicated for him to take the call and left him alone in his room.

An hour later, Skye decided to check on Jordan, as she had not heard a peep out of him since leaving his room. She knocked on his door, opening it a crack to look in and see he was sleeping peacefully. Skye retreated to her room quietly, not wanting to disturb him.

CHAPTER 11
Fight Day

SKYE'S NERVES were on end. Not only was it Jordan's first fight day, but they had not had a chance to discuss what had happened between them the previous day. Skye had to take deep breaths to keep her heart from exploding and her nerves from fraying.

"I love the way the logo for your gym and my clinic came out on Jordan's clothing and robe," Carly said, looking as nervous as Skye.

"Are you okay?" Skye frowned at her friend. There was something different about her.

"What?" Carly looked at Skye distractedly. "Oh no, I'm fine."

"Who are you looking for?" Skye asked Carly with a raised eyebrow.

"No one," Carly fobbed off Skye's question. "I should be asking you what is going on with you. You have this nervous glowing thing going on."

"Nothing," Skye said sarcastically. "Only this is Jordan's

first fight and my first boxing fight as a coach." She breathed. "He is also wearing my father's legacy on his clothing."

"Uh-huh," Carly said, unconvinced. "Let's go with that then."

"You have a very active imagination," Skye said to Carly. "Now spit it out; who are you...?" She stopped talking as Carly waved at someone, blushing. "Who has made you...?" Skye turned around and stared in disbelief. "Please tell me you are not..."

"Shush," Carly poked Skye in the back. "Nothing has happened." She hissed in Skye's ear.

"Yet," Skye whispered, finishing off the sentence for Carly. "You mean nothing has happened yet?"

"I like him, Skye," Carly whispered back.

"You really do," Skye turned to find a goofy look on her friend's usually poised face. "Oh, my word!" A huge smile spread across Skye's face. "In that case, you have my blessing."

"Thank you." Carly gave Skye's arm a little squeeze. "Now act naturally."

"I think you should be the one taking your own advice." Skye grinned teasingly at her friend.

"Skye," Carter uttered her name as he walked over to them. "How are you?"

"Hi, Carter," Skye said and hugged the tall, handsome man back. "Hey, Mason." She looked around Carter to greet his son.

"Hi, Skye, it's been a long time," Mason greeted her, smiling.

"Hi Carter," Carly smiled shyly up at him. "I'm glad you could make it."

"Hi, Carly," Carter said, staring down at her. "I am too."

Carter looked just as taken with Carly as she was with him.

"Mason," Skye said to the young man, "how would you

like to come and be part of the ringside team with me and meet the fighters?"

"Really?" Mason's eyes lit up. "Is that okay, Dad?"

"Sure, son," Carter replied, barely taking his eyes off Carly.

"Geez," Mason rolled his eyes as he followed Skye to the ring, leaving the love birds on their own. "I told my father to just ask her out already."

"You don't mind your father dating again?" Skye looked at the young man, impressed.

"No," Mason replied, drawing his brows together. "Since my mom died, my dad gave up everything to take care of me. Now that I am older and going off to college next semester, he deserves to take some time for himself and find another great love."

"Wow, Mason," said Skye, as she looked up at the young man she had known since he was a young boy. "That is very mature of you."

"Thanks, but he is a great guy and deserves someone just as great as him." Mason smiled up to where Carter and Carly were sitting. "Like Carly."

"Yeah." Skye looked back. "They do make an impressive couple."

There was one round to go, and Jordan's eye had been split open just as the bell ended the round. Carly was up in the ring as quick as a flash to patch up his eye.

"Jordan," Carly warned him. "I don't like the look of your shoulder."

"It's fine," Jordan snapped at her. "Just finish patching up my eye so I can get back out there. I need to pick up the points."

"Jordan, maybe you should listen to Carly," Skye hissed at

him. "The other fighter has noticed you favoring your weak shoulder."

"I said I'm fine," Jordan growled at the two of them, not taking his eyes off his opponent in the other corner. "Now, are you finished?" He rinsed his mouth out and put his mouthguard back in.

The bell rang, and Jordan was back in the ring. His opponent swung but missed, and Jordan countered by bringing in a hard punch with his weak arm. As his hand connected with his opponent's face, a burning pain seared through his arm, making him drop his other arm. His opponent took advantage of that and threw the winning punch.

"I want to see you first thing when you are back home tomorrow for an MRI on that arm," Carly ordered Jordan when she had finished examining him after the fight.

"I will see," said Jordan, clenching his jaw muscles as Carly deliberately pulled the bandage a bit too tight.

"If I do not see you at the clinic tomorrow, I will have no choice but to mark you as unfit to fight." Her voice brooked no argument. "And if you are ever that rude to any of your team members again, you will find yourself having to find new ones." She turned and stormed out of the locker room.

"Your attitude was uncalled for," Quinton told Jordan. "I have been with you through the worst of times. But I have got to say, the way you treated Skye after the fight was uncalled for."

"She'll get over it," Jordan said flatly. "Is everyone finished with the faffing?"

"Yeah." Quinton glared at Jordan. "Everyone is finished patching you up and trying to be there for you." He shook his head in disgust at Jordan. "I know this is a hard day for you. But it is unfair to take it out on everyone else."

"I need some time to myself," Jordan retorted, ignoring Quinton's angry taunts. "Tell Skye her service will not be needed until further notice. And inform Dr. Ice Queen that I will have an MRI whenever I am good and ready." With that, Jordan slammed the shower door in Quinton's face.

CHAPTER 12
What Happens in Vegas...

It had been four weeks since the night of the fight. Skye, Quinton, and even Carly had tried to reach out to Jordan for days after the fight, but no one had heard from him. Skye had even gone around to his house. She had tried to persuade him to go get his shoulder seen too to start training for the next fight. He had been despondent and cold, so Skye had quietly packed up her things and moved back home.

Skye's heart ached like it was bruised, but her friends kept her busy, and Pam had started at the gym. It was still early in her pregnancy; she could not fight or even spar, but she could still train. Skye was thrilled that Pam's father wanted to work with her to develop a training and diet program for pregnant sportswomen.

Liam, who was supposed to be mentored by Jordan, had come to be trained at Vic's Gym. He also helped out around the gym instead of paying for a gym membership. Vic's Gym was an exciting place as word spread about Skye and her new fantastic team at the gym. As her business started to pick up, so did the deli, Maggie's bakery, and the salon. Carter had asked Skye to partner with him and let the gym offer martial arts as well.

Bennie was going to retire soon and move down to Florida with his secret love. Skye decided she would move into the smaller apartment, and her place was going to be turned into a dojo. Everything was happening at the speed of light, which Skye was grateful for because she had no time to mope over her bruised heart.

Skye took a deep breath, her eyes filling with tears as she looked at Carly. She was dressed in a form-fitting strapless cream silk dress and was glowing—like every bride should be. Skye still could not believe that Carly and Carter's whirlwind romance had landed them in Vegas and that they were about to get married. Only Carly would want to get married in Vegas. Not at one of those cheesy quickie marriage places; no, it was a five-star hotel for the wedding.

"You look beautiful," Skye breathed. "I still cannot believe how quickly you put this wedding together."

"Well, you know I never wanted a huge wedding," Carly said, beaming. "This is the wedding I always dreamed of. And I swear my mom has baked a wedding cake for each of us each week, expecting this to happen."

"I'm not sure quite how to take that, but I'm going to go for us both being impulsive," Skye and Carly laughed. "But that is an impressive cake she made."

"I know, right?" Carly stopped what she was doing. Her expression changed as she looked at Skye. "Are you okay?"

"It was stupid of me to let myself become so involved with Jordan." Skye shrugged.

Skye smiled, remembering their recent girls' night where they had caught each other up on their love lives. Only Carly's had ended with the promise of happily ever after, whereas Skye's had once again resulted in bruises.

"He is an idiot," Carly told Skye. "Quinton said he didn't

even look at the x-rays or flinch when he was told he would need surgery."

"You did all you could, Carly," Skye said. "I still cannot believe Quinton rushed Heather off to that chapel last night and got married. Who would have thought?"

Skye and Carly looked at each remembering their surprise when Quinton had broken the news at their pre-wedding breakfast that morning.

"I am so happy for you, Carly," Skye said, hugging her friend. "And just think, you get to have a child who is already going off to college!"

It had been a beautiful ceremony, and the party was in full swing. Skye looked around at all the happy couples. Even Carly's mom had a new man in her life. It was quite shocking to find out that she and Bennie had fallen in love with each other.

Skye sighed, picking up her purse to go to the powder room. As she walked through the door of the ballroom, she bumped into someone entering the room.

"I haven't even walked through the door yet, and you are already running away from me," a familiar voice said.

Skye's head shot up, and her eyes connected with Jordan's. His face split into a smile.

"Can we talk?" he asked her.

"I was on my way out," Skye said, taking a step back to put some space between them.

"I noticed that." He gave a small laugh.

"What do you want, Jordan?" Skye sighed.

"You," Jordan said, his smile fading and the color of his eyes deepening. "All I want is you, Skye."

"Do you think you can just push me away and pull me

back in whenever you want to?" Skye's brows drew together in anger. "Do you think people are just there for when you want them to be?"

"No..." said Jordan. "I am so sorry about the way I acted. I was all twisted up inside. It was the anniversary of Wayne's death, and I felt like I had let him, my family, and you down." Jordan drew in a ragged breath and ran his head through his hair nervously. "I was so ashamed of myself because I knew that my shoulder was messed up. I just could not admit it because I felt I had something to prove."

"I'm sorry about your brother, Jordan," Skye said. "I can understand how you felt you had something to prove." Her eyes were filled with tears threatening to rush out. "But pushing me away as you did, that hurt, and I don't know if I can trust that you won't do that again." Her voice wobbled as she swallowed the lump in her throat. "Now if you will excuse me, I have to go."

"Skye," Jordan called after her, but she ignored him and kept walking.

CHAPTER 13
The Heart Wants What the Heart Wants

"SKYE," Carly followed Skye around the gym. "It's been two months since my wedding."

"Yes," Skye responded, looking at the plans in her hands. "I'm not sure about this part of the plans. Do you think the bags should rather go on that wall, and we should move the mats to that wall?"

"Skye!" Carly ripped the plans out of Skye's hands. "You have been in denial since we got back from Vegas."

"I don't know what you are talking about," Skye growled at Carly. "Now, can you please give me my plans back? I have to sign these off before tomorrow."

"Oh, forget your stupid plans," Carly said as she hid them behind her back. "Jordan is going home from the hospital today. Go and see him." She turned, rolled up the plans, and walked off with them. "If you ever want to see these again, you will go and see him." And with that, Carly left the gym.

"I can get more plans!" Skye shouted after Carly, making everyone in the gym stop and look at her. "What?" She shrugged at all of them before stomping off to her office.

"May I come in?" Quinton knocked on her office door.

"Have I ever been able to stop you from inviting yourself into my office?" Skye asked Quinton sarcastically.

"No," Quinton said earnestly. "Listen, Skye. Jordan pushed us all away; he is a complicated guy, but haven't you punished him enough?" He looked around the room. "If you continue to ignore him, you are going to have to open a flower shop." He pointed to all the flowers Jordan had sent her. "You haven't even read any of the cards."

"I've been busy; I don't have time for nonsense," Skye told Quinton. "Are you finished?" She looked to see what he was holding behind his back. "What are you up to?"

"Please read the card on this bouquet." Quinton handed Skye a bouquet of blood-red roses before turning and leaving her alone in her office.

Skye opened the card, her face splitting into a smile as she read it.

I have your plans. If you want them back, you know where to find me - Jordan

For the first time in weeks, Skye laughed. She looked around her office at the bouquets Jordan had sent her each day since the day after Carly and Carter's wedding.

"Hello," Jordan greeted Skye at the door of his house. "Fancy finding you at my door."

"Very funny," Skye said, smiling at him. "Where are my plans, Jordan?"

"No 'hello, Jordan how is your shoulder'? I'm so sorry you will not be able to box this season or maybe ever?" Jordan leaned against the door frame.

"I don't have time for this." Skye's eyes fell on his shoulder and immediately said, "I am sorry about your shoulder and your boxing career, though. It was very nice of you to petition for Liam to take your place and sponsor his training."

"He is a good kid with a bright career ahead of him," Jordan said, smiling down at Skye. "If I can't box, at least I get to stay in the game through Liam and help him fulfill his dream."

"He is doing very well, as you know." Skye gave Jordan a tight smile.

Jordan had been more than generous to both Liam and Bennie. He had also sent Skye a proposal for an underprivileged children's boxing and martial arts program he wanted to sponsor.

"Come in," Jordan invited Skye in, stepping aside for her to enter. "I was about to have some dinner. Will you at least join me, and we can discuss the children's program?"

"Will you give me back my plans if I do?" Skye asked him.

"Of course," Jordan agreed, steering her towards the dining room.

Skye stopped at the door to the room, her heart skipping a few beats. The dining room table had been set out as a romantic dinner for two. She continued walking, her nose following the smell of grilled salmon, to find all her favorite dishes waiting for her. Complete with tiramisu, she knew it could only have come from Maggie's bakery.

"Are you trying to win me over with food?" Skye turned around, smiling up at Jordan.

"That depends?" Jordan raised his eyebrows, looking at her cautiously. "Is it working?"

"Lucky for you, I'm starving," Skye admitted, allowing Jordan pull back the chair for her.

"Turns out," Jordan told her, "that I am no longer on a diet, so I am dying to try Maggie's famous tiramisu."

"And here I was thinking you were trying to win me over?" Skye laughed as they dug into the delicious meal.

Skye and Jordan had talked throughout the entire meal about his arm, Liam, the children's program, and Vic's Gym. They had moved the conversation to the lounge and shared a Merlot bottle to round off the evening.

"I will be back in a minute." Jordan excused himself.

Skye sat on the giant sofa, twirling her glass of wine. She knew she was in trouble here, and she had to stop fooling herself. She had missed Jordan terribly, and if they were going to be working together again, it was time to clear the air.

Jordan came back to the lounge carrying two rolled-up tubes of paper.

"Are those my plans?" Skye put her glass on the coffee table.

"These are," Jordan said, handing Skye the plans Carly had stolen from her. "These are plans to expand Vic's Gym into the building next door."

"I would love to do that," Skye told him. "But I don't own it, and I believe it was bought out by some corporation."

"Yes," he said, smiling at her while opening up the plans. "My corporation. I hope it is not too forward of me, but we could take Vic's Gym to another level this way."

"You want to keep the name of the gym as it is?" Skye stared at the plans in amazement.

"Of course," Jordan replied, frowning. "I would not want it any other way."

"What's this?" Skye found a small box beneath the plans Jordan had laid out on the table. She opened it, and her eyes grew huge.

"I love you, Skye, and I want to spend the rest of my life showing you how much," Jordan swallowed and got down on one knee, taking the box from her. "Will you marry me?"

"Shut up and kiss me," Skye whispered, grabbing his shirt and pulling him to her, crushing her lips against his.

Jordan maneuvered himself onto the couch, pulling her closer to him with his uninjured arm.

"Is this a yes?" Jordan asked her between kisses.

"Yes, I will marry you." Skye smiled seductively up at him before melding her lips to his again.

"I love you, Skye." Jordan pulled back to look her in the eyes. "I never want to be without you again."

"I love you too, Jordan," Skye whispered back to him before once again losing herself in his kiss.

If you enjoyed Skye and Jordan's journey from enemies to lovers, find out what happens to Kiana when she listens to her best friend and decides to drown her woes in the next ***Can't Buy a Billionaire*** story, ***One Night with the Billionaire.***

Get your copy today!

Enjoy the Preview

CHAPTER 1
A Little Mishap

KIANA HAD another few minutes left on the treadmill when her phone strapped to her arm beeped. She glanced down to see the picture of her best friend, Magda, blinking up at her. Careful not to lose her stride, Kiana hit the answer button.

"Hey," Kiana breathed as she adjusted the earphone cord.

"Hi there, stranger," Magda's cheerful voice purred through the headphones. "I was wondering if we are still on for our brunch on Saturday."

"Of course," Kiana grinned. "I look forward to our Saturday liquid brunches."

"I think after last Saturday, we should try to get a little more food this time," Magda laughed. "I did not like the morning after feeling from too many mimosas."

"Yes, but think of all the fun we had." Kiana's grin widened. "I did not realize just how well you could sing Whitney Houston songs."

"Oh, please don't remind me," Magda begged. "We can never return to that karaoke bar again, ever!"

"Why?" Kiana teased. "You won two prizes and a trophy!"

"Okay, I am going to hang up now," Magda warned her. "My cheeks are flaming still from my debut as a singer."

"Okay, okay," Kiana placated Magda. "I will say no more on the subject."

"Where are you?" Magda asked. "You sound out of breath, and it is rather loud."

"I am at the gym, where I am every day at this time," Kiana informed Magda.

"Right," Magda said. "I did not realize it was that time already. It has been such a hectic day at the boutique."

"That's a good thing, though, right?" Kiana adjusted the speed on the treadmill to a walk for her cool down. "It means your business is booming."

"I would not say booming," Magda corrected Kiana. "I would say doing extremely well."

"I hope you still have that shirt I asked you to put aside?" Kiana asked. "I will get it when I get paid next week."

"Yes," Magda assured Kiana. "It is still here waiting for you. I must go. I will call you later."

"Sure," Kiana moved her neck from side to side as she started to cool down. "Chat later." The call ended.

Kiana slowed the treadmill down a little more while doing a few deep breathing exercises before making it stop. She stood on the equipment, stretching her muscles before grabbing her towel and water to head for the locker rooms.

As Kiana rounded the corner to the locker room, her foot skidded on a puddle of water. As she tried to steady herself, her other foot slipped out, and she landed with a thud on the cold hard floor.

The back of Kiana's head connected with the tiles on the floor; as it did, it sent shockwaves of pain coursing through her entire body. Kiana felt like she was vibrating with pain as black dots floated around her eyes. She gasped for breath, having been winded by the impact of her fall. The roaring in her ears blocked out all the sounds around her.

Kiana did not know how long she had been on the floor. Time seemed to have stood still while she lay there, unable to move. When the dots cleared from her vision, a pair of strong whiskey-brown eyes stared down at her. Kiana blinked, a little confused; when she opened her eyes, the man staring down at her came into focus. She blinked again, but his handsome face was still there when her eyes opened.

Kiana could see the man's face and lips moving, but his voice sounded like he was so far away; she could hardly hear him. She shut her eyes tightly, taking in a few deep breaths. The sounds around her started to filter back into her ears as she willed her body to relax.

"Miss?" the man with stunning brown eyes called to her with concern. "Can you hear me?"

Kiana tried to speak but could not find her voice, so she nodded.

"That was quite the fall you had," the man said. "Can I help you up?"

Kiana nodded again. She managed to raise her arm towards him, but instead, he bent down and scooped her up as if she weighed nothing more than a pillow. Right now, Kiana felt like a downy pillow with feathers fluttering in her stomach being held in the man's powerful arms.

"You can bring her this way, sir," the gym manager rushed over to them. "I am so sorry about this."

"You should be," the man's deep voice rumbled through his solid chest, pressed tightly against Kiana's arm. "That spill was reported to your staff more than ten minutes ago. That pool of water should have been taken care of right away!"

"Of course, you are right, sir," the manager said apologetically. "We are a little short-staffed today due to the bad weather, and that leak has only just appeared."

"There you go," the man put Kiana down gently on the bed in the gym's infirmary. "My friend, Hayden, is a doctor; I asked one of the gym's staff to get him."

"That won't be necessary," Kiana swallowed; her throat felt dry, and her head was starting to throb. "I am sure I am ..." She tried to sit up, but the world swayed.

"No," the man shook his head and gently pushed her back on the bed. "I don't think you should be doing that. Wait for Hayden; I promise you he does not bite." The man grinned, adding a boyish charm to his devilishly handsome face.

"Well, that remains to be seen," a deep voice turned their heads towards the door.

"Hi, Hayden," the blue-eyed man greeted the tall, well-built man who stepped up to the bed.

"Thank you so much for taking time out of your training, Dr. Baxter," the manager said nervously. "Of course, we will pay for Miss Bridges' consultation and treatment."

"I am sure you will," Hayden popped his doctor's bag onto the counter next to Kiana. "Hi, I'm Hayden Baxter." He smiled at Kiana while cleaning his hands and getting ready to examine her. "Can you tell me your name?"

"Kiana," Kiana said hoarsely. Her head was pounding now. "Kiana Bridges."

Hayden looked at the manager, who nodded his head in confirmation.

"Well, that is a good start," Hayden smiled warmly at her. "How do you know Ronan here?" He took out a small flashlight.

"We don't know each other," Ronan informed Hayden. "I rushed to try and grab Miss Bridges when she slipped, but I was not quick enough."

"I was asking Miss Bridges," Hayden admonished Ronan. "Do you mind if I give you a quick examination?"

"No," Kiana shook her head.

"Okay, you two, I need you to leave the room, please," Hayden, who towered over both the men in the room, gave them a tight smile.

"I will be right outside the door," Ronan assured Kiana. "Oh, by the way, I'm Ronan." He gave Kiana a sexy smile.

"Kiana," Kiana managed a weak smile back.

Under other circumstances, she would have flirted back, but she was sure she was about to ...

Before she could stop herself, she sat up and vomited all over Ronan.

"Oh my word, Kiana," Magda helped Kiana onto the sofa. "That is a massive lump on the back of your head."

"It aches like crazy," Kiana let Magda fuss over her. "I feel like a cartoon character with a mountain of a bump protruding from my skull."

"Don't be silly," Magda laughed at Kiana's description of her lump. "You cannot see it with that thick dark hair of yours."

"Just as well, I did not go for that short haircut last week," Kiana's eyes wanted to close; she felt so sleepy. "Those pain meds are making me so drowsy."

"I will go get you a glass of water," Magda told Kiana. "You get some sleep. I will be right here when you wake up." She held up the latest novel she was reading. "That gorgeous new doctor of yours told me not to let you out of my sight for the next few days."

"Please, let's not talk about Dr. Baxter," Kiana's cheeks become colored and not from pain. "I just hope I never have to see his friend again."

"You mean the one you emptied the contents of your

stomach onto?" Magda laughed as Kiana's cheeks burned up. "Sorry, but that beats my karaoke night, hands down."

"How are you going to go to work?" Kiana's eyes started to droop as she changed the subject. She was still mortified that she had thrown upon the man who had saved her from the floor.

"Chloe and I can take turns looking after the store," Magda shrugged. "I am sure she will love getting paid to be out of the store for a couple of hours. It is only for the next two days while you are recovering."

"Thanks, Magda," Kiana smiled gratefully at her friend before her eyes closed, and she drifted off into a fitful sleep with dreams filled with images of heart-stopping brown eyes.

About the Author

Rose M. Cooper read her first novel when she was eight years old. Since then, she has read tens of novels and twice as many short stories. She, however, did not discover her special knack for writing romance fiction until a decade later.

Now a full-time author with a specialty in contemporary romance, Cooper writes sensual yet relatable love stories designed to hook her readers at first glance. She views writing as another outlet to creativity, and thus has no intentions of setting down her pen just yet. There are many intriguing love stories to be told, and Cooper is set to tell them all.

She hails from New York and currently makes her home in Copiague, New York with her husband, her black cat and her Maine Coon cat. When she is not writing, you will most certainly find her around computers or getting her nose stuck in a book.

facebook.com/RoseMaeCooper

twitter.com/rosemaecooper

instagram.com/rosemaecooper

tiktok.com/@rosemaecooper

amazon.com/author/rosemaecooper

WANT TO BE FIRST TO KNOW?!

JOIN MY NEWSLETTER!

ROSEMAECOOPER.COM/NEWSLETTER

Enjoyed the book? Please leave a review!

rosemaecooper.com/Training_the_Billionaire_book

www.ingramcontent.com/pod-product-compliance
Lightning Source LLC
LaVergne TN
LVHW091002080826
845145LV00003B/1090

* 9 7 8 1 9 5 0 3 7 8 6 1 6 *